A Wallflower's Whisper

by

Njord Kane

A Wallflower's Whisper by Njord Kane

This book is a work of fiction. Names, characters, places, and incidents either are products of the author's imagination or are used fictitiously. Any resemblance to actual persons, living or dead, events, or locales is entirely coincidental.

Published on: November 10, 2016 by Spangenhelm Publishing

Interior Design and Cover by: Njord Kane

ISBN-13: 978-1-943066-216

ISBN-10: 1943066213

1. Thriller 2. Crime 3. Mystery 4. Paranormal

First Edition.

10 9 8 7 6 5 4 3 2 1

Spangenhelm Publishing
United States

Table of Contents

Foreword

"The oldest and strongest emotion of mankind is fear, and the oldest and strongest kind of fear is fear of the unknown." ~ H.P. Lovecraft.

Chapter 1

It was sometime in the evening or even possibly the morning. The Sun was either starting to set or rise because the light outside was mixed with its brilliance of blue and white. There were smears of orange haze that crept across the horizon and painted itself along the clouds. The light made a bright green and orange glow that iced the tops of the trees and spread across the manicured landscape.

It was definitely either evening or morning.

Seeing the colors in the sky reminded Nick of a rhyme that he learned when he was young; "Red sky at night, sailors delight. Red sky in the morning, sailors warning." It was from a book he read about sailing when he was a boy.

He knew it must be sometime in the morning or in the evening. But everything was all hazy and blurred. His thoughts were in and out as if everything around him were all a dream. This made it so he wasn't sure if he was dreaming everything around him or actually seeing it.

He really wasn't sure of anything and everything around him either was blurred and fuzzy because of his eyes or because he simply could not completely wake up.

No matter how hard he tried to fight it, he couldn't stop slipping away and falling asleep. He couldn't even stay awake up long enough to remember who he was most of the time. He'd awaken, mostly, then start trying to shake the sleep off and wake up all the way. But he'd always lose and sleep would always overwhelm him.

Waking up was like trying to climb up out of a slippery muddy hole where he'd keep sliding and slipping backwards and fall back into the hole. Except, instead of a hole, he'd slip back into a slumber. He couldn't quite get his eyes to open all the way and focus on anything before he'd drift off again.

His body felt numb with a tingling sensation that ran all through it. Even his teeth feel like they were numbed. It also left an odd and indescribable taste in his mouth.

He wasn't sure why, but he just could not wake up all the way and it seemed like he laid there day in and day out. He didn't know if he'd become paralyzed and unable to move or because of some other reason. He couldn't lift his head, his arms, or even his legs. If it weren't for the occasional sting or insect bite that he felt along his backside, legs, or on his arms now and then, he'd been sure he was dead. Everything they bite or stung him, he'd get that tingling sensation going down his body before falling alseep.

Occasionally it felt like he was falling and that he wasn't able to catch himself and stop the fall. When it felt like he was falling, he'd try to reach out to catch himself, but his arms wouldn't respond. None of his body did.

Sometimes out of nowhere, he'd suddenly be blinded by a bright light that forcefully pressed its way into his eyes.

Nick hated this feeling.

It was painful and would make him feel ill. It felt as if the light were trying to pierce and press its way right through his eyes and into his skull through his eye sockets.

However, to his mercy, there was usually a heads up warning before the light would come to attack him.

Sometimes he heard the sound of some kind of bird calling. It made a sort of "sqweep, sweep, sweep" sound. At least he thought it might be a bird. He'd never really heard one that sounded like that, but he really couldn't make out what else it could be. He wasn't really sure if it even was a bird and if it was, then what kind of bird was it. He'd never seen it, only heard it and he really didn't recognize its call. It was just a squawking sound that seemed like some kind of bird that would warn him of the coming light.

The piercing light would usually come right after the bird's warning. The light would come and hit him, making his whole head and eyes suddenly pulse and throb in pain. It was as if the light would attack from nowhere and grab him out of the nothingness bliss that usually overcame him. Then the light would release him and go away, leaving him with a feeling that would make his already upset stomach feel even more nauseated.

The sting and tingling that went through his body and dragged him back into the imprisoning slumber. The light probably attracted whatever was stinging and leaving its venom in him. It was really irritating and he just hoped it wasn't feeding on him and slowly killing him.

The numb feeling was constant, besides the times when things seemed to fade out and he felt nothing. The world all seemed a blank where time was irrelevant and seemed to skip around.

Yet time did pass by, he was sure of it. It had to, but he wasn't sure if he was even alive anymore. But he must still be alive, otherwise he wouldn't wonder about it.

'Do the dead know they're dead?'

He also wondered if someone was keeping him alive for some odd reason. How was he existing? This thought often haunted him when he was semi consciousness enough to think about it.

Or was this what death was? It all seemed like he wasn't really dead, yet he wasn't really alive either. It seemed like he was stuck somewhere in the middle of life and death.

"Where am I?"

Sometimes he could see the horizon of the world he once knew pass by overhead as clouds drifted by. He'd see the treetops and sometimes the grassy earth. However, it was usually only the tree tops and sky that he'd see. The scene would often alter in its color from time to time. Sometimes it was all blue with patches of white and smears of yellow.

Most of the time, everything was all ablur to him. Faint shapeless blurs of color that made no sense at all.

He seemed to exist in a mist that was a constant haze of frozen time that jumped around in brief fuzzy scenes.

Nick knew it was the colors of the sky that he'd often see. But to add to his confusion, it was often different than the last time he remembered seeing it. Day, night, or some confusing place in between were always changing with a blink of an eye.

He seemed to always be phasing in and out of consciousness. One moment, he'd see the sky and drift off in thought before fading back into nothingness and then again he'd awaken trying to remember... anything.

Trying to figure out who he was and where he was. He never could figure anything out. Was he laying on the ground dying somewhere? Sometimes there was nothing but darkness or mixed with a strange blurry whiteness. Sometimes the world revealed itself to him, but only for a whisper of a moment before returning to the darkness.

Most of the time it just all seemed like a horrible twisted dream as if he were in either Hell, Purgatory, or some kind of Limbo. Tormenting him by bringing him in and out consciousness.

He could see the darkened sky now. It had dark gray cloud with smears of green in them.

"Was it just dawn or was it dusk? Did I just fade off again?"

Now and then the world would suddenly lighten up for

a quick second and reveal ever changing shapes and dimensions as dancing across the sky.

It was lightning that did it from a storm that was passing over. Yes, lightning. He was fairly sure, because he could hear its muffled grumble of thunder that followed shortly behind the brilliant display of chaos athwart the celestial sky. He could also hear the wind picking up outside and the periodic swishing sound that it made as it swept its way across the trees.

Yes, it was lightning and that was a storm. He was aware of that much going on now. Whatever 'now' was.

Strangely enough, he often heard his name being called in the storm's wind. They were coming for him and he knew it. How he knew it or why was just as much a mystery to him as everything else was. But they called out to him and he could feel their presence in the shadows watching him. Watching him from the shadows within the shadows.

"Watchers in the shadows."

Occasionally he'd see one of them pass along the nothingness before him in an unexpected blurred haze. Sometimes he heard them whisper amongst themselves. They were definitely there and he wasn't just imagining them in his hazy stupor. He was sure of it.

Their whispers were too much of a murmur to make out what they were saying to each other. Their voices always seemed to trail off and fade away as they also faded back into the shadows of his memory. Leaving everything as a forgotten haze until he would awaken again, trying to solve the mystery.

Time was lost and just a myth now. Nothing seemed real anymore.

But now he could hear the bird calling out its warning. The light was coming to attack him again. He was thankful for the bird's warning, but felt apprehensive as he heard it makes its call, 'tweep, tweep, tweep, tweep.'

He mentally braced for that awful, angry light that would attack and sicken him.

The sudden flash of the light hit him as it always did. It pressed its way deep into his head. He hated it. He had no idea why it attacked him or where it came from. Thankfully, the bird always seen it coming and squawked its warning for him.

He could also hear the shadows whispering again.

'What are they saying?'

Suddenly something stung him in the leg. It wasn't a small sting like an ant or mosquito, this was something larger like a scorpion perhaps. He felt the poison from its sting run up his leg and start its way up through his body.

The light released him from its torturing embrace, but the sick feeling still ran through him and cause his stomach to sickly churn. He could feel the poison running through him, making its way to his head.

He felt tired, so very tired. He wanted to vomit as the unknown taste entered his mouth and made him ill. He couldn't keep awake any longer. He could feel himself slipping off again from the accursed poison of whatever felt compelled to keep stinging him on a regular basis.

Everything was fazing out again and he could hear nothing but ringing in his ears now. Nothing but slumbering blackness and the dull hum of stillness.

Chapter 2

For as long as he could remember, Nick Runarstein had always been afraid of the dark. It didn't matter whether it was day or night, the shadows within the darkness always made him feel very uneasy and apprehensive.

He always got a deep feeling pressing inside him that warned him not to venture into the beckoning of the darkness. Something within him knew to be wary.

The shadows would gently call out to him from within their dark, dense places and whisper to his curiosity. Reassuring him that it would be 'okay' to venture within their cloak of darkness. He'd often see or hear things that nobody else seemed to hear or see. Or, at least, that other people didn't want to admit to seeing or hearing.

He knew something unseen was hiding and lurked within the very darkness of the shadows themselves. It always kept him on his guard as it hinted that something indeed was there with him. He always felt like he was being watched and he never felt completely alone, even when he knew for sure there was nobody else around.

This beckoning really never allowed him to feel alone as it would faintly whisper its presence through the ringing silence from out of the darkness. He often wondered how silence could even do that. Drown out the world around you and then overcome you into another.

Indeed the quiet can become quite deafening in its haunting persistence.

Nick would always try to drown out the overwhelming silence when it reached out to him. He'd try drown it out with various forms of white noise and attempt to break loose from its haunting trance. Even then, he'd still hear its faint whisper reaching out to him from out of nowhere.

It was a very distant-like, hushed sound that seemed like it was far away, yet seemed very close. He never really even heard it, just sort of 'felt' it. A feeling that was very close, close enough to touch him.. Too close.

It seemed like it was whispering either to him or to someone else, he could never quite tell. He was never even sure if he'd heard anything in the first place. As soon as he thought he noticed it, it would be gone without even the faintest trace. This is what made him not even sure that he'd heard anything at all.

Nick was really never able to completely hear or understand the faint whispers when he was sure he was hearing them. Sometimes when he tried to listen, it would be just too faint to understand and then it would always gently drifted off and fade away into the drums of silence.

Even without hearing the whispering, he always sensed that something was just in the shadows of the other room watching him. That was the feeling the bothered him the most. Sensing something in the darkened corners or in the shadows of the room he was in. Feeling them, or it, hiding behind the door, in the closet, or the darkened hallway.

Whatever it was, it always seemed as if it just lurked there and stared at him while it hid in the shadows. He always felt it watching him and softly whispering incomprehensibly.

It made him feel cold and concerned about, not only his body or general well being, but it seemed like his very inner essence of existence and he was instinctively afraid of it. It made him feel as if he were in some kind of serious peril.

'Who or what was in the shadows and why did they watch me?' he thought.

Nick's mind often raced with these unanswered questions and he often wondered why 'it' or 'they' wouldn't leave him alone. He had no idea what they wanted from him and couldn't understand why it seemed like the very semi-presence of whatever lurked in the darkness would make his very soul feel a coldness and fear that he couldn't quite describe. Not even to himself.

It didn't matter what he was doing, Nick instantly knew when "it" or "they" were close. He could feel a coldness growing near him that drifted up to him as if something were creeping up behind him. He could feel it peer over his shoulder. Part of his body would get chilled and make his hair stand on their ends. It felt as if a cold breeze just blew gently across the back of his neck. A chill that ran past his neck and down his shoulders to his arms that went all the way to the bone. The hairs on his arms felt as if they stood up while goose bumps formed and tingled across his skin.

There was no denying it, he knew something was in there with him. He wasn't alone and he could feel it. Nick sensed it creeping up from behind him. Even the air around him seemed to change with a lingering cold and still reach. It felt close enough to touch as it soundlessly whispered behind his ear. It made his skin crawl as he half expected something unseen to suddenly touch him from behind.

Of course, there was never anything there when he could no longer help himself and look. No matter how cunningly he tried to be to sneak a glimpse or how fast he turned his head to catch *'them or it'* off guard. Mysteriously it seemed like it was there and yet it was not.

He knew he wasn't crazy. He'd seen the uneasiness in other people when they felt the presence too. Yes, he knew they definitely felt it too. They'd get a glimpse in the corner of their eye or the same feeling that they were being watched too. He'd seen other people blankly stare at nothing in the darkness, searching for whatever unseen being lurked there.

They'd feign bravery if they were ever caught nervously looking into the dark nothingness and try to play it off. They didn't want anyone to know that they were scared of something that wasn't even there. Such a childish notion and far be it for anyone to be thought of as being afraid of empty shadows. The nonsense about spooks and things that went bump in the night.

Yet something indeed lurked within the shadows.

14

There was only the cold emptiness that mocked anyone for looking when they tried. It deceived everyone into believing that it was merely their imagination and would cause them to laugh at their own foolishness for even thinking anything was there.

But it quietly returned the very moment you became relaxed and confident of its absence. Sneakingly and stealthily peeping again at you from within the shadows of a darkened corner, watching. Always watching from the obscurity of the shadows. Even up in the darkened corners, they would always sink back into the dark oblivion whenever you felt them there. A dense shadow from within the darkness of the very shadows themselves.

There was a dark presence that lurked there and it neither allowed itself to be completely seen nor would it take complete form before it would fade back into the shadow's darkness. Being sensed, but never seen.

Nick still remembered when he started to really notice them. He was just a little boy and it was difficult for a small child to understand it. He remembered being scared one night in his bedroom. The hall light was on and his bedroom door was slightly ajar to keep the room partially illuminated from total darkness. Little Nick was in his bed with the covers pulled up to his chin as he laid there awake and wide-eyed. He was frightened by the darkness that seemed to be growing in the shadowy corners of the room.

He had felt a chill slowly creep over him. Even though it was summer time, his toes were cold and strangely, it felt very chilly around him. It felt as if he was in a room with

the air conditioner turned up too high. But they didn't have
any kind air conditioning and even though he was under a
light blanket, the cold still seemed to creep its way in and
brush over him. Fingers of cold that felt like his bed sheet
was slowly being pulled off from his body while he laid in
bed. A sudden wave of tingling coolness that made him
shudder as a brush of cold air gently traveled across his
body and made goose bumps form.

It wasn't really like the room was too cold though. It
was more like the air around him had suddenly changed
and made him shiver as his awareness around him
heightened.

All he could do was fearfully lay in his bed, watching
the shadows in the corners of his room slowly grow larger.
It was barely even noticeable, but he noticed. It seemed
darker in the room than it had been just a second ago. Then
suddenly without any kind of warning, he felt his bed
move.

"Did the bed just move? It felt like it just slightly moved
like someone had gently bumped it." He thought to himself.

Nick laid there frozen, petrified with fear and not
moving a single muscle as he quietly listened.

All his senses were heightened as he stared out into the
nothingness in front of him.

After a moment or so, when he decided that he'd
probably just imagined it, he felt the bed move again.
Suddenly and ever so slightly, the bed had gently shook.
He was sure it moved this time. Nick quickly sat up,

bracing himself on the bed and again froze in fear. He
didn't know what to do. His mind raced in denial, "was it a
weak earthquake or just his overactive imagination?"

The bed shook again, ever so slightly. He could barely
feel it moving, but he definitely felt it move. He looked
down at the bed and watched it,waiting to see if it shook
again. He still wasn't sure if it was just his bed shaking or if
it was the whole house trembling?

He felt the bed gently shake again, but still wasn't sure if
it was his bed or the house. It shook yet again, but this time
he heard a faint voice coming from inside the bed saying,
"help, I'm trapped in the mattress!"

Instantly he sprung to his knees and moved to the
opposite end of the bed. He felt the blood rushing through
his body and the thumping of his heart racing all the way to
his ears, making him immediately feel faint and panicked
all at the same time. He skin tingled pale as his heart beat
so hard it felt like it was going to come right out of his
chest.

"I know I didn't just hear that," he said to himself.

Again the bed shook and a faint but more pronounced,
"help me," came from inside the bed mattress right in front
of where he was peering!

Nick's hair stood on end as his eyes widened even more
from sheer panic. Like a frightened cat, he leapt from the
bed and flew across the room towards the door, which was
still slightly ajar allowing the light from the hallway in. It
looked like his feet didn't even touch the floor as he raced

out of the bedroom and down the hall into the living room where his mother and her boyfriend "Chuck" were at.

They were sitting in the living room on the couch, drinking beer. Both Chuck and his mother turned simultaneously and looked at Nick, startled from him suddenly darting down the hallway and appearing around the corner into the living room where they were seated. Their eyes were widened from the surprise at his sudden appearance and from the obvious look of fright on Nick's face.

He just stood there looking at them. He couldn't even speak. His heart was pounding so hard, he could even feel it pulsing in his lips.

After a moment, Nick's mother repositioned herself on the couch to face Nick while leaning towards him and asked, "what's the matter, Nicky? Why aren't you in bed?"

Chuck, whom was sitting right next to her, also turned and said, "Listen to your mother and go back to bed."

Nick just stood there looking at them and then backed away slightly and quickly shook his head "no," indicating that he did not want to go back in there.

There was no way he was going back in there, he thought to himself. He didn't care what they said or did to him.

Chuck tilted his head slightly to the side, changing his approach and asked him, "What's the matter? Why are you scared to go back into your room?"

Nick had already been through this song and dance many times before. First, he'd say that he'd heard or seen something, then they'd tell him that he didn't or that he was just making things up to avoid going to bed.

Nick didn't answer Chuck's question and just stood there timidly looking down towards the floor.

His mother then said, "you can't be afraid of the dark forever. There's nothing different in there, then when it's *not* dark."

She was wrong, Nick thought to himself. Something *was* in there and he knew they weren't going to believe him. Besides, something deep inside him, told him that whatever was there in the dark was also there when the light was on. It didn't matter.

Chuck turned and leaned forward, setting his beer can down on the cork drink coaster that was on the coffee table and stood up. He walked around the couch and stood in front of Nick, placing his hands on his shoulders before kneeling down to get eye level with him.

"You don't need to be scared of ghosts. I'm not going to argue with you if they are real or not. All I am saying is think about, ghosts can walk through doors and walls, right?"

Nick looked up at him timidly and responded with a weak sounding, "yes."

Chuck smiled and stood back up, turned around and took a couple steps away from Nick before turning around to face him again.

"Well then ghosts can't hurt you then."

Nick looked at him inquisitively, not quite sure what he meant.

Chuck continued as he walked back towards Nick and said, "if a ghost tried to get you, it would just go through you wouldn't it?"

Nick cocked his head to the side, still unsure what Chuck was trying to explain.

Holding his arms out, Chuck tried to mimic a ghost lunging forward and said, "you see, if a ghost tried to get you it would just go through you. There is no way it can even get you."

Chuck then pretended to go through Nick as if he was a ghost himself by stepping around him and continuing walking forward. He stopped, turned around and did it again.

After one more final demonstration, Chuck turned around and said, "see, a ghost can't even grab you. It would just go right through you if it tried."

Chuck looked at Nick's mother and winked while Nick soaked it all in.

He did make sense after all, Nick thought. If a ghost goes through solid objects like walls and they're transparent, then they really can't do anything in the material world. If they did try to grab you, they'd just go through you.

Nick's face lit up when he was satisfied with this

rationalization. It made sense to him and he was no longer afraid. He no reason to be afraid realizing that ghosts couldn't actually do anything to him.

Seeing Nick's face lighten up and his posture relax a little, Chuck knew his rationalization made sense to him. So he walked back to the couch and returned to his seat, grabbing his can of beer before he leaned back on the couch to the original position before Nick came running in. As he sat down, Nick's mother took the cue and got up from her seat and came around the couch collecting Nick up and walked him back to bed.

She comfortingly rubbed his back as they walked back down the hallway towards his bedroom,

"See, there's nothing to be afraid of." She said reassuring him.

Nick went back into his room as she followed behind him and got back into his bed. She pulled the covers over him and tucked him in for the night. She smiled at him as she brushed some of his hair to the side and leaned down to kiss him on the forehead

"Good night, sweetie."

"G'night Mommy."

"No more running out of your room. Get a good night's sleep."

She stood up and turned to leave the room, blowing one last 'good night' kiss at him as she stepped out of his room. Before she'd left, she stopped momentarily to close the bedroom door a little, leaving it slightly ajar so the hall light would illuminate in before walking back down the hallway towards the living room.

Feeling a new sense of confidence, Nick got comfortable in his bed and closed his eyes to gently drift off to sleep. But as he laid in his bed trying to go to sleep, he heard a soft whisper near his ear from inside the bed say, "I'm still here."

Nick never forgot that night as a little boy. It was several years ago, but it had horrified him to the point that he developed a deep fear of the darkness and whatever it was that hid within its shadows.

Nobody could tell him that nothing was there or that he was just imagining it. He'd experienced something being there and no matter how much everyone told him that it didn't happen or that it was just his imagination going wild, simply hadn't any idea what they were talking about.

But after all, how could someone explain something like that happening to them and have anyone believe them in the first place. Their first thought would be that the person was either trying to play a prank on them, trying to scare them or that they'd literally lost their senses and needed psychiatric help.

Since then, after being punished for screaming out of his bedroom after being told to go to bed, he been ridiculed and he never told the story about that night to anyone ever again. No matter how much he tried to forget about it happening, every time he was in the darkness he'd instantly be reminded that he wasn't alone in it.

Chapter 3

The morning had come quickly. Last night's rainstorm had not lasted very long and the sun was already out erasing all traces that it had even passed through during the night. Nick woke up to the alarm clock's rude announcement that it was already time to get up and go to work.

He worked for his father's roofing company resurfacing flat top roofs through the summer and now the summer was coming to an end with the school year starting up. The majority of the roofing crew, minus his foreman Tom, attending school during the week, so they pretty much only worked late afternoons and on the weekends now. They'd already got the majority of the apartment complex's roofs resurfaced during the summer and there were only a few roofs left to do.

The current schedule was now set up for them to work most afternoons and every weekend to get the last roofs done. The roofing contract was nearly complete, so they weren't overly constrained for time.

Nick knew because it wasn't raining and the rain from

last night was short lived, that they'd be on the roof today. They'd start the day by sweeping off last night's rain water from the flat top roof. This was necessary in order to clear the water puddles and dry it off so they could start resurfacing it. It would dry and ready to be worked by either later today or tomorrow.

Nick got out of bed and dressed for work. After putting his work boots on he went downstairs to get something to eat before heading out. When he reached the bottom of the carpeted steps and turned to walk towards the kitchen, but his dad's bedroom door opened and his dad poked his head out just as he was passing.

"Why are you already on the roof pushing rain water off?"

"I had just got up. I'm on my way now."

"The Sun's already out, you're wasting daylight. Better get your ass on that roof and get the water off."

Being that his dad was already up and on the prowl, Nick decided it would be best to skip breakfast and just head out the door and go to work.

"I'm going now." Nick said as he headed out the front door and closed it behind him before his dad could answer back.

His dad and a long time drinking buddy of his had partnered together and started the roofing company that Nick worked for. His partner's sons and Nick were the roofing company's compulsory labor pool.

It only took him a couple of minutes to walk over to the job site because the roofs that they were working on were also a part of the apartment complex that they lived in. The building they were working on today was less than a block away.

Nick arrived and as expected nobody else was there yet. He knew they'd along any moment though. He could guarantee, if his dad was already up barking about the roof, then no doubt he was on the phone putting a fire under the other guy's asses to hurry up and get out there.

Knowing the rest of the crew would be there any moment, Nick sat down on a parking curb and took out the crushed pack of cigarettes that he had in the back pocket of his pants. He carefully opened the smashed pack and took one out. They were bent and a little flattened into a square shape, but in general they were okay and not broken. He lit one up and put the remaining pack carefully back in his pocket, trying not to crush them any further than they already were. Nick sat there smoking his cigarette as he patiently waited and daydreamed as he looked out into the horizon.

As he sat there on the parking curb, Steve, his friend and neighbor that he'd got to know over the summer came walking around the corner. Steve's apartment was the one next to the building he was roofing today.

Steve noticed Nick sitting on the parking curb smoking and hollered, "You know those things will kill ya don't ya?"

Nick looked up at him, smirking and said, "You don't wanna live forever do you?"

Upon that wisecrack, Steve swiftly replied, "Ha! Yes I do!"

Steve walked up to where Nick was sitting.

"Hey man, you gotta work today?"

"Yeah, my dad's already up and on it. I couldn't get out the door fast enough. I'm just waiting for the rest of the guys to get here. I'm sure my dad's already called them and they're on their way."

Steve laughed. "Yeah, I've met your dad once before. Once was enough. He's probably already chewed them up and down over the phone asking them why they aren't already at work. I have to go to work today too."

"Working breakfast menu, huh."

"Yeah, the new guy didn't last. I'm back to nights and mornings again until they get someone else."

"You know you can always join us up on the roof. Better pay."

"No fucking way, dude. I've met your dad. I'd rather sweat n a grill for lower pay than put up with that shit."

Just then Tom's truck came around the corner.

"Ha! He's already chased them out of their beds. They don't look like they're even awake yet."

Steve laughed, shaking his head.

"Yeah, I definitely prefer my job to ya'lls. The pay is lower, but at least my boss is nice to me...most of the time."

Nick crushed his cigarette into the ground with his boot and stood up as the other guys pulled up and parked the truck.

"Well, there they are. Looks like it's time for me to get to work."

Well dude, I have to get to work too. I'll catch ya later."

Steve started walking off towards his car before turning around and asking, "Are you coming over tonight? I'm going to pick up some cold beers on my way home."

"Yeah. Sounds good, I'll be there."

Steve walked to his car and Nick walked to where Tom had parked his truck. Nick noticed that Tom was alone and the other guys weren't with him. He didn't say anything, but he hoped that they were still going to show up. It wouldn't be the first time he got screwed and ended up sweeping the water off a roof all by himself.

Tom got out of his truck. "Hey bud, are ya ready to squeegee some water off the roof."

He laughed at his own remark and turned to untie the extension ladder that was on top of his truck.

"Help me get this ladder set so we can get started. Ken and Dave, those pussies will be here in a few minutes. They couldn't get their asses out of bed in time, so I made them walk."

Nick walked around to the back of Tom's truck and unsecured the back end of the extension ladder from the ladder rack and helped him lift it off as they carried it over to the base of the building.

When they set the ladder down, Tom said, "I got this, grab the brooms and squeegees out of the back of my truck."

Nick walked back over to Tom's truck and gathered up the brooms and squeegees from the bed of the truck while Tom set the ladder up for them to get up on the roof. He carried the tools over to the ladder and set the squeegees on the ground while he carried the brooms up the ladder to the roof. Tom grabbed the squeegees and went up the ladder behind Nick.

Just as they got on top of the roof, they heard David call out to them from below.

"Hey bitch! Why didn't you wait and give us a ride?"

He was obviously talking to Tom, whom had just told Nick minutes ago that he made them walk to work. It wasn't a long walk. After all, they lived in the center of the apartment complex, which was only a couple blocks away.

Tom started laughing and then nudged Nick saying, "See what I mean, they're pussies."

He continued laughing as he walked to the roof's edge and then called down to Ken and David, whom had now reached the base of the ladder.

"Y'all better get yer asses up here before Nick's or your dad sees that you're not working."

Tom was Ken and David's uncle. His brother-in-law, their dad, had given him the job as foreman and a place to live until he got back on his feet. Tom had served six years in the Navy and when he got out, had trouble finding a job and maintaining a place of his own.

Being that he lived with Ken and David, he always messed with them and gave them a hard time for his own personal amusement. Nothing harsh really, just pranks and general comical mischief.

They climbed up the ladder and joined Tom and Nick on the roof. Tom handed them each a squeegee as soon as they stepped on the roof and they all immediately got started sweeping and squeegeeing the water off the roof. Without a word needing to be said, they all knew it was best to work as fast as they could and get the water off. Particularly if they could get it done before any of the 'bosses' showed up.

They worked and pushed the water off on the back side of the building where there weren't any windows or doors. This way they didn't inadvertently get anyone wet from the water they were pushing off the roof. If any of them did, it was a guarantee that they'd all definitely hear about it.

It took them about two hours to get the rain water off the roof and they were almost done when Nick's dad showed up with a couple of mops.

He told them to mop up any remaining water residue until it was completely dry before any of them even though about going to lunch. He figured while they were at lunch the sun would dry the roof the rest of the way and then they could get started laying the re-roof down.

They quickly mopped up the remaining water residue off the roof and left for for lunch break.

"Where do you guys want to go for lunch?" David asked.

"I don't care, I'm starved. I didn't get to eat any breakfast before starting work." Nick said.

"None of us got to eat. You dad called our house and started chewing us out immediately because we were still in bed." David said.

"That's because you losers think you can sleep in when you know you have to go to work." Tom said.

"Hey, you were in bed too." David pointed out, nudging Tom.

Ken laughed, nodding his head in agreement.

"Well, I still got out here on time."

"Yeah and ditched us, made us walk out here."

"That's because you guys were moving like molasses water."

"Well, lets go grab a burger." David said while rubbing his stomach.

"Hell with that, I'm not eating that shit. You guys can if you want. I'm getting some real food."

"Where are you taking us?"

"I'm not taking you guys anywhere, I'm walking to the smorgasbord. All you can eat and it's real food, not fast food. You know, home cooked meals on a real plate."

"Walking? Why are we walking? Why don't you just give us a ride?" David protested.

"Because, you guys don't buy my gas and I'm not as lazy as y'all. It's right there, I can see the building from here. There's no reason to drive when I can just cut through the grass and walk there."

With that statement, Tom began walking towards the all you can eat restaurant, leaving David, Ken, and Nick standing there pondering whether or not to follow or go elsewhere. All of them had driver's licenses, but none of them had a vehicle of their own. Their choices were limited.

"Well, let's go." Ken announced as he began walking.

"Aren't you coming, Nick?" David asked as he turned to follow Ken.

"I have to swing by my place real quick and grab my wallet. I'll meet you there."

Nick walked back to his apartment and was relieved that nobody was home. He quickly ran up the stairs towards his room, being careful not to trip on the carpet steps. For some reason he was always tripping over his own feet when going up those stairs. His feet would catch on the edge of a carpeted step and make him fly face first into the steps.

He entered his room and grabbed his wallet off the dresser. He didn't know why he forgot it this morning, he never forget his wallet. Those were two things that he never lost in his life. His wallet and his keys.

Nick secured his wallet in his back pocket and turned to leave his room to go back downstairs and catch up with the guys at the restaurant. However, just as he was about to step out of the bedroom into the short hallway leading to the stairs, he heard someone whisper his name behind him.

"Niiick."

Nick turned around to see who was there, but nobody was there. He did notice that his room was a bit darker than usual. He kept a heavy drape over the patio door window that was in his room. It blocked out most of the outside light and there was only had a mere low wattage light-bulb on the ceiling that lit up the room. The ceiling light made the room more of a creepy orange, rather than actually illuminating it. The room was always kind of darkened and in shadow.

It was something that always made Nick feel uncomfortable, but his dad and stepmother wouldn't let him put in a brighter light bulb. They informed him that he could get a brighter, higher watt light bulb when he was the one paying the electric bill. With it being a darkened room was one of the main reasons he didn't hang out in there very much at all. Even still, it was unusually darker now than usual.

Nick scanned the room and seen absolutely nobody in there. Yet, he couldn't shake the feeling that he was being watched. Not in the cliché creepy kind of way you always hear about. He felt like someone was standing in the corner of the room hiding in the shadows and staring at him. Almost as if I could actually see someone, but he couldn't see anyone. Nobody was there, even though it strongly felt like someone was there. So strong of a feeling, he actually felt their eyes on him.

Nick shook it off. He was probably just imagining it. He didn't have time for his imagination to play tricks on him anyways. He had to hustle out of here and get to the restaurant so he could get something to eat before they returned to work. It would make for a much longer day to work all day on an empty stomach.

Nick left the room and started heading down the stairs. Just as he was about halfway down, he heard his bedroom door slam shut. It startled him and made his heart skip a beat or two. Not to mention, he nearly tripped on the steps of the stairs when it happened.

It was probably a breeze, Nick rationalized as he briefly stood on the steps and listened. A breeze from where he don't know. The patio door in his room was locked shut. He never opened it, he wasn't allowed to open it. It was secured in place by a screw preventing it from being opened. But maybe another window upstairs was open, like his stepsister's bedroom window or something.

No matter, there was no sense in getting creeped out of trifles that were probably nothing. His wasn't about to let his imagination get the best of him. Nor did he have time to play detective over something so trivial as his door slamming shut.

All these thoughts of rationalization raced through his

mind as he hurried and made his way down the rest of the stairs. When he reached for the front door to go out, it slowly opened right in front of him.

"Wow, more creeps. Ha! I'm not fooled by this one bit." He nervously said aloud to himself.

Now he knew his imagination was in overdrive. In his haste to get in and get his wallet, he obviously didn't shut the front door all the way.

Looking at the door and accepting this explanation, Nick laughed at himself for being spooked by it.

Nick stepped outside while digging in his packet for his keys and reached to shut the door so he could lock it. But before he was able to grab the door handle, the door slammed shut by itself. He would have blamed this on the wind too, had he not heard the deadbolt snap itself locked as well.

Nick just stood there for a moment staring blankly at the door with his keys still in his hand. Hmm, this was very suspicious. 'Good prank,' he thought to himself. Obviously his stepsister must be home and was trying to scare him.

“Good one, Monika, you almost had me.” He said at the door as he turned and started walking away. He didn't have time to play around though, he had to get going.

The restaurant Tom wanted to go to was only a couple blocks up on the small business strip on the main street next to the apartment complex. It was a short walk and would only take him a few minutes to get there. Nick decided that he would take the shortcut through the middle

36

of the complex.

This route, would also make sure he'd pass by the complex's swimming pool. Girls dressed in bikinis were usually already laying out in the sun there and of course he wanted the opportunity to see them. Especially if Laura and the other girls were there and they usually were.

Nick had met Laura during the summer and immediately had a huge crush on her. Which was unfortunate, because she was his friend Steve's girlfriend.

He crossed through the complex and weaved his way to the pool and lo and behold, there they were. The girls were by the pool as he'd hoped for. Nick tried to not be obvious looking at them as he walked by.

Laura was there with her girlfriends, Nina and Renee, whom he had just recently met. They were all sunbathing beside the apartment complex's swimming pool.

He noticed Laura was laying prone on her stomach on one of those white chaise lounge chairs. From the gleam of the sun reflecting from her back, shoulders, and legs, he could tell she was smothered in suntan oil as she laid there absorbing the sun's rays.

He could also smell the aroma of coconut all the way over where he was as he passed by. Her skin was already a bronzed tan from sunbathing regularly at the pool. He liked how her suntan accented her short light brown hair. To him, it made her even more attractive.

She laid on her stomach as did Nina next to her with their bikini tops unfastened so their backs could tan without getting the tell-tale tan lines. His eyes jumped back and forth between the two of them, as he admired their buttocks. Nick could see the tan lines already across their backs from previous tanning sessions when they had their bikini tops fastened.

Even though all three girls were extremely attractive, he couldn't help looking at Laura the most. She was the most beautiful thing he'd ever laid eyes upon.

Nick slowed his pace as he walked by the pool as his eyes drooled over them. He realized that one of the girls, Renee, noticed him slowing his pace as he was walking past. 'So much for walking by, not being obvious and thought of as a perv,' he thought.

Renee looked up at him from behind the magazine she was reading after noticing his slowed pace as he looked at them while passing the pool's gates. Teasing Nick, she slightly spread her legs apart and flashed her bikini covered crotch at him. Seeing that he got a quick peek, she quickly closed her legs and returned to her original sitting position. After which,she looked at him over her sunglasses and smirked mischievously with her deep, wet, red glossy lips.

Nick briefly stumbled walking, but quickly recovered hoping nobody noticed him nearly trip over his own feet.

However, Renee seen him stumble and giggled. She nudged the lounge chair next to her with her foot, getting the other girl's attention and whispered something to them that he couldn't hear.

The two other girls, Laura and Nina, whom were both

laying on their stomachs, turned their heads and looked at Nick through their dark sunglasses as he continued walking past the pool.

Laura, situated on the far left, reached up and briefly pulled her sunglasses down, smiling and giving Nick a quick wink.

Seeing her smile at him, Nick instantly smiled back without even realizing he did it and was instantly embarrassed. He felt his heart start to race and his face warm as he began to blush. He was embarrassed how obvious he was and was even more embarrassed when he figured out that she knew that he secretly had a crush on her. Nothing ever had been said or implied, but he could just tell she knew.

Still walking and embarrassed by his blushing, Nick stepped off the sidewalk and stumbled again as he stepped back on the road.

All three girls laughed and waved at him while Nina called out mockingly, *"Hiiii Niiiick!"*

The girls all giggled as he blushed even harder as he waved back at them.

Having passed the gates by the pool, Nick noticed Ken and David up a ways ahead of him down the road. He quickened his pace to catch up to them. They had a head start on him but because they were such slow walkers, they didn't get very far ahead of him.

After jogging up the road a bit, he finally caught up to them before they turned the corner towards the restaurant.

They arrived at the "all you can eat" smorgasbord restaurant. It was Tom's favorite place on Earth. It wasn't a bad deal, the restaurant charged a person a flat price to enter, so you could return to the buffet line as many times as you wished. You just had to always making sure to grabbed a clean plate each time you went back to the buffet table for seconds or thirds (or even fourths and fifths if you liked).

The restaurant kept stacks of plates at the end of a long steam table. The steam table had rows of stainless steel bins full of prepared food that was set up for self service. Staff were on the opposite side of the steam table 'at the ready' to maintain cleanliness and tend to the food bin as needed. Their job was simply to make sure the food bins were always full and presentable. Refilling or changing them as needed.

At the end of the long steam table was where the meat was cut and placed upon your plate upon request. An employee at the end of the table stood in front of roast beef and smoked ham, cutting slices for those whom wanted some. Next to him, stood another employee that was cutting slices of roasted chicken or turkey to serve. The dessert and beverage table had attendants as well.

Indubitably, it was the place to go if you were famished and had a huge appetite. The selection was vast and of course, you were welcome to eat all that you could.

The restaurant's lights were dimmer than the light outside and it took a moment for their eyes to adjust. The shades over the windows outside were drawn, keeping it darker and cooler inside the restaurant than it was outside. After a brief wait in line to pay first, they went in to feast heartily upon the vast variety of foods offered.

They got in line at the steam table and found Tom already at the steam table piling food on his plate. They all got their plates and quickly caught up to him.

"Jeez dude, I knew you were hungry but you don't have to pile up that much food on your plate. You can come back for more." Ken said as he stood next to Tom.

"This way I don't have to make as many trips."

They continued working their way down the buffet line, piling up their plates in the buffet line.

"Nick, did you notice the girls by the swimming pool before you caught up to us?"

"Yeah, I seen them sunbathing by the pool."

"Yeah he did," Ken joked. "I seen how he was walking fast until he walked past the pool and then he slowed way down."

They all laughed at Nick's expense. He already knew he actions were obvious from the girl's reaction when he walked by the pool. It just embarrassed him more that his co-workers had noticed it too.

"Yeah, I 'admired' them as I walked by."

"Hahaha, he 'admired' them." David said while laughing. "I bet you did."

This just made them all laugh more, even making Nick

laugh at himself.

"Do you know them?" David asked.

Nick just shrugged his shoulders, implying that he didn't and busied himself with the buffet table.

"Aww bullshit, dude. I heard them say your name." Ken quickly countered.

"Eh, I've talked to them a couple of times. That's all."

Nick wasn't going to tell them that he already knew the girls. If he did, he knew they'd hound him to introduce them to the girls and he knew they didn't have the honor to leave the girls alone as all three of them already had boyfriends.

Besides, Nick had hopes for Laura himself and didn't want any of them ruining it for him if he ever got the chance. He wouldn't step on Steve's toes and hit on his girl, but if their relationship didn't work out, Nick wanted a chance with her without anyone else messing it up.

Returning from their lunch break, they made sure they walked past the swimming pool where the girls had been earlier on their way back to the work site. However the girls had already left, so they returned to the work site and spent the remainder of the day laying that building's roofing on.

It was a hot day, plus the hot roofing tar reflected the heat back at them and only made it hotter. They worked quickly and had finished the roof about midway through the afternoon. It was the hottest time of the day, which also made it an ideal time to quit for the day. After cleaning and putting their tools up and cleaning the tar off themselves, They left work and parted ways for the rest of the day.

Nick went home and took a long shower. He had a difficult time getting the turpentine and tar off his skin. They'd used turpentine to clean the tar off their skin, which really didn't work that well and burned their skin as they tried. Regardless of his efforts, Nick was always stained of it. He hated how it made his hands look dirty and unless someone realized that it was just tar stains from roofing, he appeared as 'filthy' to them no matter what.

It was just an additional thing that made him hate roofing.

Nick's hands were simply stained brownish and also along his forearms all the way up to his elbows there was a filthy looking spotty pattern. There was also a stain on his forehead from where he'd wiped the sweat off his brow while working and got some tar on it without realizing it.

Nick hated roofing passionately, but there wasn't much he could do about it. He worked for his dad and couldn't just quit. His dad didn't give him a choice, just announced that he was working for him and that was it.

There were only a few roofs left on this contract anyways from what he knew. The roof jobs for this apartment complex would soon be done and he wouldn't have to worry about roofing anymore. He could get a different job as soon as they were done.

Nick looked forward to that.

After getting as much of the roofing tar off as he could, he got dressed and headed out to hang out with Steve for the evening. He'd told him this morning when he'd seen him that he would. Besides after spending the day melting on a hot roof, spending some time relaxing in the air conditioning and doing pretty much nothing was a welcomed invitation.

Additionally, hopefully he'd get to spend some time with Laura as well. Even though she was off the dating list because she was Steve's girlfriend, Nick still liked being with her. He enjoyed her company and spent as much time with her as he could without stepping on Steve's toes or space.

Chapter 4

Nick spent much of the evening at Steve's apartment hanging out with Steve and Laura. They had pretty much wasted the evening away by listening to loud music and drinking beer. Nick was starting to get quite good at playing the drinking game, "quarters."

It was a game where one player would bounce a coin (usually a quarter) off the table and try to get it to bounce into a glass full of beer. If the coin bounced into the glass of beer, the person that bounced it in got to choose who drank it. If they missed after three tries, then they had to drink it.

Nick had already drank quite a few beers before he'd finally got the hang of it. Before the night was over, he'd become practiced enough that he was able bounce the coin off the table and get it into the glass nearly every time.

When he got home late that night, he was luckily that has dad wasn't home yet. This meant that he wasn't locked out of the apartment and was able to stealth his way into bed without being noticed. Nick crawled into his bed and passed out for the night still in his clothes.

The next morning Nick found out that they didn't have to work because the supply house didn't have everything in stock that was ordered to get the roof done today. He knew this because he woke up to hearing his dad screaming on the phone downstairs at the construction supply house.

So basically, they would have to wait a day or so before working again. Nick didn't mind at all. He hated working on the roofs anyway.

Because he didn't have to work, he took a quick shower, got dressed and left the apartment. His dad stared at the TV and paid him no never-mind as he went out the door. Not even mentioning that they didn't have to work today.

Nick walked over to hang out at Steve and Laura's apartment again. He remembered Steve mentioning last night that he had the day off and didn't have to work. He'd told Nick to stop by after he got off work. Being that Nick didn't have to work now, he figured he'd just show up earlier. He was sure Steve wouldn't mind.

Nick walked over to Steve's apartment and knocked on the door. Steve answered, letting him in.

"Hey man, you're here early. No work today?"

"Naw. I guess they didn't have all our supplies ready. I heard my dad yelling at them on the phone when I got up."

"Well, a day is off is a day off. You're just in time to work out with me."

"Nick looked at Steve with an eyebrow up.

"Work out? I already get a work out on those roofs."

Steve laughed and said, "No, I mean pump some iron and form your muscles. Get buff dude."

Steve liked to lift weights and had a bench press in his living room set up where most people would have a television. He was setting up his weights when Nick arrived.

The first thing Nick noticed was that Steve had a lot of weights set up on bench bar. He couldn't tell how much weight, but it was two large ones and two medium sized ones. The bar Steve used look like it was weighted as well. He had it all set up on his bench press and ready to go.

After he tinkered with the weights a bit more, Steve positioned himself on the weight bench.

"Spot me, dude." Steve said as he adjusted himself under the bar better so he could lift the weights evenly.

Nick had never "spotted" anyone before, but he'd seen it done before on many occasions and knew what he was expected to do. He just wasn't sure he'd be able to lift the weights up if Steve wasn't able to. They looked pretty heavy and appeared to be more than Nick could handle.

"Spot you? Dude, how much weight do you have on that thing? I don't know if I'd be able to lift it up if you can't."

Steve chuckled. "Dude, you can do it. Just believe in yourself."

Nick looked at the weights on the bar.

"How much do you have on there?' Nick asked as he

looked at the weights on the bar.

Steve sat up on the bench and looked at them.

"let's see, I have two fifties on each end and two twenties. That comes to 280 pounds," he said after calculating it in his head.

Steve re-positioned himself on the weight bench again.

"I haven't lifted that much before, but I want to try it now while I have someone here that can help spot me if I have trouble."

"Dude, I don't didn't think I'd be able to lift that much weight off you if you have any trouble."

Steve laughed and said, "it'll be okay, all you have to do it make sure I keep straight and help me pull it up if I have any trouble."

Nick still had doubts. Steve could see it written all over his face.

"You don't have to lift it yourself, only help me lift it up if I have any trouble with it," he said trying to reassure Nick.

With that, Steve re-positioned himself on the bench and grabbed the weight bar. He made several puffs of air and then with a mighty groan lifted the weighed bar up off the bench rack and started to bring it down to his chest. His face began to turn from bright to dark red as he strained with the weight.

He blurted out,"spot" and Nick quickly grabbed ahold

of the weight in the center of the bar and helped him lift it back on its rack.

Steve sat up and let out a long breath of air. After a moment, embarrassed he said, "I forgot the bar is weighted at twenty pounds too."

"That makes the total three hundred pounds."

Nick smirked and said, "I told you it looked like it was too much."

Steve laughed and stood up, saying, "let's take some off from each side."

"We'll take off forty pounds and make it an even two-sixty," he added.

Steve removed the clip that held the weights in place so they wouldn't slide off and pointed to the other side and said, "pull one of those twenties off."

Nick reached over and pulled off the safety clip on the other side of the bar to slid one of the weights off. He could see the "20 Pounds" marked on the side. He slid the weight off and set it down on the floor, leaning it against a couple other weights of different sizes.

Steve did the same and put the safety clip back on.

"Make sure you put the clip back. We don't want any of the weights slipping off. It's a fast way to get hurt."

Nick put the clip on and secured the weights in place.

Steve sat back down on the bench and positioned himself to lift them once again.

"I know I can do two-sixty," he said as he reached up and took a firm hold of the bar.

He let out a couple quick puffs of air and lifted the weight bar up and off the bench rack. He slowly lifted it down to his chest and then lifted it back up. He repeated this, doing five reps then pushed the weights up and set the bar back down on the rack.

Steve stared up at the ceiling for a moment and then let out a victory yell and sat up in the bench.

He turned and looked at Nick.

Smiling, he said, "I can sometimes get seven of those in at two-sixty. Soon, I'll be able to do the three hundred."

Steve got up from the bench and grabbed a towel he had on the floor and wiped the sweat from the bacl of his neck.

"Get down there and try it out." he said, motioning to the weight bench.

"No way, I've never lifted weights before in my life. I probably could only lift a hundred or so."

Steve laughed at this remark and said, "Dude, you work on those roofs all day. You probably have way more muscle than you think you do."

Nick just smiled and shook his head in disagreement.

"I bet there's an incredible hulk hidden somewhere under that skinny frame of yours," he said attempting to encourage Nick to try to lift the weights.

"That's okay. Maybe some other time."

Realizing Nick wasn't going to budge from his conviction and not try to lift any weights, Steve walked into the kitchen.

"You wanna beer, Dude?"

"Sure. I gotta use the bathroom real quick."

Steve nodded as Nick walked down the hall to use the downstairs bathroom.

As soon as he entered the bathroom, Nick instantly could smell Laura's perfume lingering in the air. It made him pause a moment as he took in her fragrance and thought of her wearing her skimpy bikini bathing suit.

His thought train was immediately interrupted when he heard Steve in the other room turn on his stereo. Nick could feel the bathroom walls and floor vibrate from the music blasting through. He silently giggled when he considered what the neighbors must be thinking when Steve cranked up his stereo system like that. Luckily, most of them were probably out for the day at work or something, he mused as he took care of his business.

He finished using the toilet and went to wash his hands. He looked up in the mirror and noticed that the bathroom was getting darker behind him. Startled, Nick turned to look behind him but the lighting in the bathroom was normal. The lights hadn't dimmed in even the slightest way. He turned and looked back in the mirror again, but in its refection, the room had indeed grown darker. Everything in the mirror's reflection had gotten darker than it was a moment ago. So much had it darkened that the light reflecting in it was only fractional. As if the bathroom was only lit by a single candle.

Nick looked around uncomfortably, noticing that the light around him was still normal. It was only happening in the reflection of the mirror for some strange reason. It gave him the chills and he tried to ignore it by looking down as he finished washing his hands.

He turned around to dry his hands on the towel that was hanging behind him. Just as he turned, he heard his name whispered behind him.

"Nick."

It was coming from the direction of the mirror. Even stranger about it was the fact that Steve had the music blasting so loud that it was literally making the walls vibrate. But when Nick heard the faint whisper, he heard it so clearly, it was as if he'd heard in dead silence.

Nick decided to ignore it. Obviously the music was too loud to even hear such a thing. He could barely hear himself think, much less hear some imaginary whisper.

He turned towards the bathroom door to leave and could see the mirror in the corner of his eye. The mirror was pitch black as if the bathroom were in complete darkness.

Trying to ignore it, he tried to turn the bathroom door knob, but it wouldn't turn. The door knob was seized. He tried to turn it the other way, jiggling it to the left and then to the right, even pulling on the door to no avail.

Panic was setting in and he tried to calm himself. Nick looked at the doorknob, maybe he accidentally locked it and was just being foolish. So easily spooked by an obvious hallucination of thinking the mirror had darkened. He turned the little lever on the doorknob to see if it was locked or not.

It wasn't locked, even though the doorknob wouldn't turn.

He turned the lever and locked it then tried to turn the doorknob, but again to no avail. He unlocked it and tried again. His efforts were becoming more rushed and panicked as he tugged on the door trying to open it.

The music was blaring through the walls, He could feel it pounding into his ears and felt it vibrate the bathroom door as began feebly pounding on it and yelling, trying to get Steve's attention.

Steve couldn't hear him through the loud music.

After a brief moment of trying, Nick stopped. He knew Steve couldn't hear him and he'd have to wait until the song ended and try again during that moment of silence before the next song came on.

Nick's panic grew as he felt a strong presence behind him. He nervously looked behind him, but seen nothing. The bathroom was still well lit and he was alone in there. He could see the mirror was still darkened in the corner of his eye as he tried not looking at it.

He turned back to the door and tried to open it again, but the door knob was still seized and wouldn't budge.

Feeling panicked and in peril, Nick continued his feeble attempts to get out of the bathroom by trying to force the door knob to turn. After a few more tires, he finally gave up with a feeling of defeat. All he could do was wait for the blaring music to stop so he could call out for Steve to help him get out of bathroom.

Finally, he heard the volume of the music tone down as the song ended. Nick renewed his efforts to get the door knob to turn and open, but it was still seized shut. Then suddenly, just before he was about to pound on the door and call out to get Steve's attention, the door opened.

Nick opened the bathroom door the rest of the way and looked out into the hall. He was expecting to see Steve standing there laughing at him from pulling a prank and holding the door knob from the other side of the door the whole time. But he wasn't there, nobody was there.

The music started again as Steve put on a different song. Nick seen that he was in the living room and seen that there was no way he could have been holding the doorknob and got back there that fast.

Nick walked into the living room and joined Steve, whom was crouched down in front of his stereo system. The music was loudly blasting again. Steve noticed him walking in and turned down the music enough so he could speak.

Laughing he said, "it cranks insane, doesn't it!"

Nick laughed with him and agreed by saying, "yeah it does, I felt it all the way in the bathroom. It made the walls and floor vibrate."

Steve laughed even harder when he heard Nick say that.

Nick didn't mention what had happened to him in the bathroom. He didn't want Steve to think he was crazy. Besides, he also rationalize that if Steve did prank him, he didn't want him to know that he'd 'got him.' Nick could take a joke as well as the next person, but he seriously didn't think Steve could have made the mirror do what it did. Not to mention the strong feeling he'd had of a presence in the bathroom with him and hearing his name whispered.

Besides, if Steve's apartment was haunted, he probably didn't want to know about it. But most probable was that Nick seriously doubted that Steve would believe him anyways. Nick figured Steve would most likely think that he was some kind of freak or nutcase if he did tell him what happened. As far as Nick was concerned, it was best to just keep it to himself and forget about it ever happening.

After a few moments, Steve gave a wide grin as he turned down the music again.

"Last week, someone called the cops on me for having the music too loud."

Nick laughed with him about this.

"It doesn't surprise me, how loud you crank it all the time."

They both laughed even more when Steve turned the stereo volume back up again.

After the song ended, Steve turned the stereo back down and sat down next to Nick on the couch.

"My machinist classes end this week."

"Oh really? I knew you went to trade school, I just didn't know for what."

"Yeah, it was for machinist. It seemed the better choice, as far as everything they offered."

"So, are classes about to start again? Do you get a break in between?"

"Oh no, nothing like that, Dude. I'm done. I actually finished classes out last week. I graduate next week and that's it, I'm done."

"Are you going to start working in your new trade now?"

"Definitely! I'm done working on a grill, dude. I've already got a job lined up back home."

"Home? You're not from here?"

"No, I just moved here to go to school. I'm going back to Missouri. There's a machine shop that's already hired me."

"Is Laura going with you?"

"No way dude. We're not serious."

"I'm sorry to hear that. I thought you guys were doing great." Nick remarked, but secretly he was glad. That meant he'd soon have a chance for Laura himself.

"Naw, it was just a brief fling, if you know what I mean."

"How did she take it?"

"Well,..um,.I haven't told her yet."

"Dude!"

Steve just smiled and shrugged his shoulders.

"You knew all this time?"

"Well, yeah. Of course I did. This was my last semester and I landed the job over a month ago when I went home to visit my parents."

Nick just looked at him. He didn't like the idea of seeing a friend hurting another friend, especially when it was going to be Laura, but he kept his opinion to himself.

"Dude, you gotta promise me you're not going to say anything."

He looked at Nick with pleading eyes. "I plan to tell her when the time is right."

"Alright man, I believe you. I won't say a word."

"Promise?"

"Yeah, I promise."

Nick didn't like the idea of Steve bailing on her like that and felt he was being put on the spot for not saying anything.

Steve got up from the couch and stepped over to the stereo to put on another song. As soon as the music started playing, he turned the volume up again, but not as loud as before. After of a moment of looking through his music collection, he waved Nick over to come join him.

"You pick out the next one, I have to take a leak."

Nick nodded and started thumbing through the choices.

While Steve was in the bathroom, Nick considered the possibility of dating Laura after Steve left. He wasn't going to let Steve know this though. He didn't want his friend to know he had feelings for his girlfriend.

Even though, he was getting ready to ditch her without notice, no matter what Steve said and Nick knew it.

Nick had mixed feelings. He was concerned about how Laura was going to take finding out that Steve was leaving. He knew she'd be heartbroken and even more so when she figured out that Steve was just using her. Yet at the same time, he was happy to learn that he'd have the opportunity and with her after Steve moved away.

In all honesty, he was elated to learn that Laura would soon be available to date.

Indeed he wanted the opportunity to be with Laura ever since he'd laid eyes on her. He'd instantly fell for her. But she was untouchable because she was already seeing Steve. Because of this, Nick had to keep his feelings for her a secret.

A secret he could soon reveal when the time was right.

Nick turned around and nearly jumped out of his skin. Laura and Nina had come in and snuck up behind him. They were standing directly behind him when he turned around. The music had been so loud that he didn't hear the front door open when they came in.

Steve was standing in the hallway laughing. He'd seen them come in but noticed that Nick hadn't and didn't say anything as they snuck up behind him.

The girls were laughing too.

"Well hello ladies!" Nick said with a surprised look on his face.

"Hi Nick," they both said in almost unison, making them laugh even more.

Laura walked over and turned the stereo down a little so they could hear each other talk. Nick noticed immediately that the girls were both in their bikini bathing suits. He especially noticed when Laura bent over to turn the stereo volume down. Nina caught him looking at Laura's backside and smiled at him with a twinkle in her eye. Seeing that she'd caught him looking. Nick smiled back. He could only shrug his shoulders and look away shyly, slightly blushing.

"We're only here for a minute to grab a snack and drink before we head back." Laura said as she briefly embraced Steve and then headed to the kitchen with Nina in tow.

It was pretty much how the girls spent their days, laying out in the sun and working on their tans.

Nick smiled with a young man's usual dirty mind as he looked at Nina's too small bathing suit as she walked past him. His imagination went even further as to what she probably looked like without it.

'If only,' he thought, *'if only.'*

The girls grabbed some grapes out of the refrigerator and a couple of soda pops and headed back out the door.

Before going out the door, Laura turned towards Nick and asked, "are you coming over tonight? I'm cooking spaghetti and you're more than welcome to come over and join us."

"Yeah dude, come and have dinner with us tonight."

"Thanks, I'd like that, but I'm not sure if I'll be able to make it or not. I'm suppose to go to John and Sarah's and help them move a washing machine."

"Okay, there will be plenty

The girls went out the door as Nick sat back down on the couch. He was disappointed that the wood privacy fence around the front patio blocked his view from seeing their backsides as they walked back to the pool.

Steve walked back into the living room after retrieving another beer from the refrigerator.

"So you're going to John and Sarah's tonight?"

"Yeah, john asked me a couple days ago if I could help him move a washing machine from upstairs. He said he's getting a new one today."

"His old one busted?"

"Yeah, I think so."

"Bummer." He said as he took a drink of his beer. "Looks

like you get a work out today after all!"

"Yeah, right." said Nick.

Chapter 5

Later that day, Nick went to John and Sarah's apartment. Sarah was behind in her laundry, so it wasn't long until Nick and John got started wrestling the broken washing machine down the stairs.

As they wrestled it down the steps, Sarah had to follow behind them with a towel mopping up. The old washing machine was leaking water as they moved it and was leaving a water trail all the way down the stairs.

They moved it outside and took a short break before they were going to haul new one upstairs. It was setting in the middle of the living room and was all ready to go. Sarah couldn't wait to try it out.

Just as we started wrestling the new washing machine up the stairs when there was a knock at the front door.

Sarah answered the door while Nick and John continued negotiating with the stairs as they muscled the new washing machine up it. Thankfully, it was a bit lighter than the old one. Most likely because the old one still had some water in it that John failed to drain.

Sarah's cousin, Jeshua, was at the door. Sarah let him in.

"Hey Jeshua, come on in. You're just in time. John and Nick are carrying my new washing machine upstairs."

"Hey guys!" Jeshua hollered up the stairs to greeting them as he came inside.

"Do you want to help them carry the washing machine up?" Sarah asked him.

Before he could answer, John yelled down the stairs at Sarah, "It's okay hun, we don't need any help. We've almost got it up the steps."

Nick noticed John's reply was a little to quick and looked at him with a questioning raised eyebrow. John just rolled his eyes and smiled.

They got the new machine to the top of the stairs and then moved it into place in the utility room. It only took John a minute to connect the hoses and plug it in.

While they were in the utility room and out of earshot, John explained his wife's cousin to Nick.

"He's a bit of a religious fanatic. I hate it when he comes over. It's always Jesus this and Jesus that."

"Oh yes, I know the type."

"Yeah, I'm pretty sure he wouldn't have volunteered to help. But if he did, he would have been more int he way. In case you were wondering why I quickly cut off Sarah when she was asking him to help."

"Oh don't worry man, you don't have to explain yourself

to me."

John and Nick went back downstairs and found Jeshua and Sarah sitting on the couch talking to each other.

"Nick, this is my cousin, Jeshua Eiferer."

"Hello Jeshua, it's nice to meet you." Nick said as he extended his hand to him.

He stood up and took Nick's hand. Nick immediately noticed that Jeshua had one of those limp clammy grips of weakness when he shook his hand. He seemed like he was very polite and was also well groomed, like one of those Baptist kids. He wore loafers and was dressed in khaki slacks and a long sleeved shirt, which he had buttoned all the way to the top with the collar nicely starched. Jeshua appeared to be around twenty years old and was very friendly and soft spoken.

John invited him into the parlor where we were hanging out and socializing before we decided to move the washing machines. John showed him the knight's helmet that we had been admiring earlier. He had bought it last weekend at a swap meet somewhere out in the country. John liked to collect medieval things, but his collection was mainly of war memorabilia. He had a glass display cabinet which he kept most of his collection safely locked behind the glass.

His collection consisted mostly of old British and French bayonets, gas masks, and mess kits from World War One. A World War Two Japanese rifle that was rusted in parts that he was gradually restoring part by part. In the corner of the room, stood an old store mannequin that was partially dressed in medieval knight's armor, now complete with the helm he had just purchased.

As interested in the memorabilia as John and Nick were, Jeshua didn't seem to share their enthusiasm for the tools and relics of war too much.

"You know, the Lord doesn't like war. His is a message of peace."

John and Nick just shared a look without saying a word.

Jeshua apparently was a born again christian, as he'd mentioned being saved a number of times already.

Trying to veer the conversation away from religion, Sarah asked him about his girlfriend.

"How are you and you're girlfriend doing?"

"She's doing well, thank you."

"I heard she had a kid already"

"Yeah, the Lord had blessed her with a son. He's five years old."

"Oh that's nice. How has be been taking you moving in with him and his mother?"

"He doesn't seem to care too much about that. He's a good boy. He's just..."

"Just what?"

"Well, I don't want to sound like a crazy person."

John and Nick secreted a quick look between each other. They were both thinking, 'too late' as Jeshua continued.

"But I think her son is evil or something."

"Evil?" Sarah said, bewildered. "What do you mean?"

"Well, this is going to sound crazy, but I think the child is possessed."

Everyone in the room just looked blankly at him after he'd said that, not knowing really how to respond to something like that.

"Small kids, especially five year olds, can be wild at times but I wouldn't go as far as saying he was evil." Sarah tried to explain to him.

"Oh, I understand what you're saying. He's actually not as 'wild' as some kids can be. He's really well behaved.

"Well, then what's the matter?"

"There's just something 'off' or 'not right' about him. Like I said, it's not that he really misbehaves or anything like that. I just get the feeling that something isn't right about him."

"Dude, are you serious?" John said. He couldn't hold his tongue anymore.

Jeshua got defensive and tried to explain himself. "Recently he made a ceramic pencil holder in his art class at school."

"Oh yeah, that's a nice," Sarah pointed out.

"Well, yeah. His mother was all proud of him too."

"I bet she was. It's always nice when your kids make

you something."

"The only problem was it just seemed eerie. Like something was wrong with the pencil holder he'd made."

"Anything a five year old makes isn't going to be perfect work of art. After all, he's young and just learning to work with his hands."

"Oh, it wasn't that bad. The kid actually did a pretty good job making it. It's just that it was a little creepy looking."

"Creepy looking?"

"It looked,...well, it looked satanic" he said.

"Dude, are serious? I hope you didn't say anything to the kid. They're very impressionable at that age. They need praise at that age for their attempts."

"His mother accepted the gift of course and praised him for it as any mother would."

"That's good"

"But even she felt very uneasy about the thing. Even though it was made by her son and she was proud of him, it gave her the creeps."

"That scary, huh. Well, maybe he's got a future in making scary things." John remarked. Sarah gave him 'the look' to stop it.

"When he'd brought it home from school and gave it to her, she displayed it on the end table."

"That must've made him feel proud. I always put things my daughter gives me up too."

"It still gave her the creeps and made her uneasy. A couple of weeks passed by and she moved it from the end table in the living room where it was displayed and put it on top of the refrigerator. She thought nothing of it again."

Nobody said anything.

"I mean, it was creepy and really didn't go with her living room décor anyways. She only had it displayed to make her son happy, but only after it seemed like he was no longer paying any attention to it. She figured it would be a good time to put it up somewhere else."

"We understand, there's no reason to explain your actions."

"The next morning when she got up and went into the living room, she noticed it setting there on the end table, where it had previously been placed before."

John laughed and said, "The kid noticed it was moved and put it back."

Jeshua's face became more serious as he continued with his story. "She didn't think much of it either at first."

"Perhaps he'd seen it missing from being on the end table and looked for it."

"Oh, I agree, he could have found it on top of the refrigerator and climbed on a dining chair to retrieve it."

Everyone nodded in agreement.

"She assumed the same thing and went about her usual morning routines. She got her son up out of bed, got him ready and took him to school."

Jeshua paused a moment to take a drink from the glass of iced tea Sarah had got him earlier.

"When she got back from dropping him off at school, she took the ceramic object and this time she put it in the cabinet above the refrigerator. You know, somewhere he wouldn't be able to reach it and because he couldn't see it, he wouldn't even know it was up there."

"That makes sense, the kid probably seen it on top of the refrigerator and got it down to put it back where he felt it belonged." John pointed out.

"I don't know, on top of the refrigerator is awfully high and he's pretty short. He's only five." Jeshua tried to stress.

"Any kid could climb up using a chair or something to get it off from on top of the refrigerator. Just because he's five, don't think he's not resourceful. You'd be surprised how kids can climb or get into things."

"Well, it stayed up there for a few days and was pretty much forgotten. At least until we started moving."

"Oh yes, I almost forgot, you guys were moving into a new apartment. You'll have to invite me over when you get all moved in." Sarah said.

"We will, it's a very nice apartment, much larger than the one we had before. Anyways, when we were packing boxes in the kitchen and clearing out the cabinets, wrapping up the glassware and everything; she took the ceramic pencil holder from the cabinet above the refrigerator and threw it away in the garbage."

Sarah interrupted him, "you guys threw away his art project?"

Jeshua nodded as he shamefully looked down.

"Aw poor kid," she said. "He made that special for his mommy," shaking her head.

He nodded his head and then defended her action by saying, "well, she kept it out on display for a couple weeks and did praise him for such a good job. Her getting rid of it was secretive so he wouldn't know and be hurt."

Sarah raised an eyebrow at him, but said nothing more.

"When she threw it in the trash, she put it in under some other trash. You know, so he wouldn't be see or accidentally find it. The plan was to pretend it was misplaced during the move if he ever asked about it."

Everyone nodded, letting him know they understood what he meant.

"Personally, I really didn't know what the big deal is." John said. "I mean after all, it's just a little kid's art project. We've all hung our kid's drawing or something up on the refrigerator. I really don't understand why this ceramic thing or whatever bothers you guys so much. But to each their own, I suppose."

The room got quiet and Jeshua could tell that everyone thought he was overreacting.

"Don't get me wrong, there's more to it than it just looking creepy. After tossing it in the trash, she continued wrapping the remaining glassware in paper and packed them into boxes. She even personally taped and sealed all the boxes shut, so nothing would fall out or anything."

Jeshua's face grew more concerned as he continued telling his story.

"Her son never came home since the boxes were being packed. Her mother picked him up from school and he stayed with her while we moved. You know, spending time with grandma and all."

"Oh yeah, that's always the wisest move with small children." Sarah said.

"We made our move into the new apartment and then began unpacking the boxes. When we unpacked the kitchen boxes, in the very first box she opened. Right on top of everything else was the ceramic object her son made in art class that she'd thrown away."

Everyone looked at each other in disbelief.

Seeing the look on everybody's face he exclaimed, "Yeah! It was carefully wrapped in newspaper, just like all the other glassware and it was also setting on top of everything else in the box. We couldn't believe it!"

He stood up, continuing with his voice seemly more alarmed.

"There was no way it could have got there. She'd personally packed the box herself."

At this point it was obvious to everyone that he was scared.

"She personally wrapped each and every item with old newspaper that went into the box and then she sealed it shut by taping the box folds down. Nobody else was there. There was absolutely no way that thing could have got in the box, especially wrapped in paper."

Sarah let out a surprised, "Wow."

He nodded at her and said, "Nobody else was home or in the apartment when she'd done all this. She was alone."

Nick asked, "What's the big deal about this pencil holder anyways?"

"It just seemed like it was...evil. I can't explain it. There's just something about this kid that scares me."

"I don't mean to point at a child or anything like that. It's just something I really can't explain."

Jeshua stood back up. He looked down for a moment, deep in thought before he spoke again.

"Last night, I woke up in the middle of the night because I heard a noise in the room. I sat up in the bed and looked around in the room trying to see what it was as my eyes adjusted. When I looked at the end of the bed, I seen him."

"Who?" Nick asked.

"Him. Her son. He was just sitting there on the floor with his back to me. I figured something was wrong or he wasn't feeling well or something, so I called out to him and asked him if he was okay."

He stopped a moment to take a drink of tea.

"That's when it happened."

"What happened?"

"He just turned around and I swear on the bible, that his eyes," he said, looking visibly horrified at this point. "They looked like…"

Nick finished his sentence, "like black pools."

"Yeah, like black pools! How did you know?"

"Does her son have very pale skin with curly, almost white hair?"

"Yes, he does."

Jeshua paused a moment with a puzzled look on his face. He knew he didn't describe the kid in a way, except by saying how old the kid was. He knew there was no way this guy could know what his girlfriend's kid looked like.

"That's so weird, how do you know this? What are you, some kind of psychic or something?"

"No," Nick said, "I had this dream a few years ago that played out the same way that you said what happened to you last night."

"A dream?"

"Yes, it was very strange. It rattled me so much, I actually remember it, even now."

"Wow. Yeah, I understand that. I've had those weird dreams that shake you up so bad you don't forget them. Where you wake up from it and you're not sure if it was real or just a dream."

"Yeah, it was just like that. In my dream, it was like I was awake, but still dreaming. I wasn't sure if it was real and I was awake or just dreaming it all."

"I know what ya mean. I've had those."

"In my dream, I heard giggling towards the end of the bed and when I looked, there was a boy sitting on the floor. He had really pale skin and he had curly hair that was almost white. I mean really white hair."

Jeshua looked at Nick with stunned look on his face. John and Sarah also had surprised looks on their faces.

After a moment, Jeshua finally spoke and asked, "what happened next?"

"In my dream, this kid turned around and looked at me and his eyes were black. I mean, they were icy black, if such a thing exists. It scared the hell out of me."

Jeshua looked horrified after Nick said this.

Sarah's curiosity was completely sparked now. She looked at John and then at Nick with shocked look on her face.

"Whoa, hang on a minute. Tell me more about this dream, Nick."

Nick nodded and then explained, "A couple of years ago

I was living on the streets. Before coming to live with my dad, I bounced from house to house after my mom died."

"That's terrible." Sarah said with a saddened look.

Nick nodded in agreement and then shrugged his shoulders and continued telling his story.

"One day, I ran into my older sister, Jeanie, when I was walking down the street. She'd seen the state I was in and told me to come home with her and stay with her at her place. She's a few years older than me and already had her own apartment on the other side of town."

"I hadn't seen her in a long time and pretty much lost contact with her a few years ago when she and my mom had a falling out. Anyways, she invited me to come stay with her and drove us to her apartment."

"That night, she had to work and said I could use her bed while she wasn't there, otherwise I could sleep on the couch. I remember her bed was very comfortable and the first real bed that I'd slept in for a while. It was a welcomed change and I had quickly fell asleep. I mean, I fell asleep had almost the very second I laid down. I was exhausted. I remember leaving the bedroom door slightly open to let the kitchen light to light the room so it wasn't pitch black."

"I remember being asleep, yet it felt like the air was thick and sort of hazy. It was weird, it didn't seem right."

"Almost choking me" he added.

"I could see the shadows in the corners of the room slowly growing around me. They were getting larger and darker by the minute."

They all looked at Nick puzzled.

"The room gradually got darker, as if the kitchen light that was coming in through the door was being slowly dimmed or how it gets darker when the door's slowly being closed. It was gradually and noticeably getting darker in the room."

"I knew I was asleep and that the light wasn't actually being dimmed or the room's door wasn't being closed. And strangely, as this was happening, I was also aware it all could be an illusion from fatigue."

"I watched the room slowly get darker and I wasn't even sure if I was awake or just dreaming it all. Even still, as it was happening I was trying to rationalize it to myself that I'd been so overcome with exhaustion from being out in the cold so long and that I desperately needed rest. It was strange, because if I was asleep, I was actually rationalize it all away as an illusion due to fatigue."

"So, you were overcome with exhaustion," John said. "That would definitely cause you to hallucinate or have a nightmare."

Sarah and Jeshua both nodded in agreement.

"It seemed like the room was closing in around me with the shadows on the wall and ceiling advancing all around me."

"It's hard to explain," Nick tried to point out.

"Then the darkness was on me and I fell into a deep

sleep. I mean I crashed-out hard. Yet, it felt like I was still half aware of everything around me and half in a state of some kind of dreamlike whimsy. If that's even possible."

They all nodded when he looked up to let him know they understood what he was trying to explain.

"Go on, tell us the rest."

"Like I said, even though I was asleep, it was like I was wide awake and conscious of everything around me. I looked around the room and could see that the door was still slightly open. I wasn't sure how I was looking around the room, because I was sure that I was asleep."

"It was like I was having a dream about me being awake and not dreaming it. I can't really explain it."

Everyone in room nodded their heads.

"Suddenly, as I was looking around, the shadows receded back into their places and I could slightly hear the muffle of my sister's television in the other room. I didn't even notice that I wasn't able to hear it when the room darkened."

"As I looked around, it seemed like nothing had changed and again I wasn't sure if I were dreaming or not. But things still didn't quite seem as they should be. It was then that I thought I heard a hushed giggle coming from the floor on the other end of the bed."

"I wasn't really sure if I heard anything or not until I heard it again. It was very faint and hushed, but I could tell it was a giggle."

80

"It was strange, because it sounded just like a small child's giggle. I sat up in the bed and leaned forward to see what it was. I looked over the side of the bed and seen a small child sitting o the floor. He had his back to me."

Knowing where this was going, Sarah gasped an "oh my god," holding her hand to her mouth with wide eyes.

Nick nodded in agreement.

"It was a small boy, perhaps four or five years old. He was looking down at something in front of him. I couldn't tell what it was, because he had his back to me."

Jeshua, responded in a nervous voice, "really?"

Nick nodded.

"What did he look like?" Jeshua nervously asked.

"He had blonde curly hair. Natural curls and his hair wasn't just blonde, it was really more white than anything. He was only wearing a pair of pajama pants and I could see that his skin was pale white, like an albino's."

Sarah asked, "What was he doing?"

"He was just sitting there bent over as if he was occupied with some sort of toy on the floor. I couldn't see what he was doing though. But strangely, the kid seemed familiar to me. I felt like I knew who this child was or that he was somehow acquainted with me."

Jeshua was almost pure white by this time. He looked as if he had seen a ghost or something.

"I looked at this kid, he was just sitting there with his

back still turned towards me looking down at something on the floor. But here's the even weirder part. As I tried to look closer at this kid the room seemed to phase out into a haze as I moved closer towards him. I wanted to see what he was doing and what he had in his hands. My curiosity was overwhelming, I had to know who this kid was and why was he in here."

"Even though I was dreaming the whole thing, as real as it all seemed, I still knew I was only dreaming it all. It was puzzling, it was like somehow I was supposed to know that I was only dreaming."

"Then all of a sudden it was all quiet. The background noise of the television in the other room was gone all of a sudden. It got all quiet and I started hear ringing in my ears. It was pulsating and growing louder as I crept closer to the end of the bed to see what the kid was doing. I was determined to look at him and see what he had in his hands."

"The closer I got to the end of the bed and nearer to this kid, the more I began to feet labored. It was like I was very tired and my body felt heavier. Everything seemed like it was moving in slow motion. King of like being held back or burdened by something, slowing me down."

"Everything was in slow motion, like on TV?"

"No, it was more like when you're trying to walk in a swimming pool." Nick said.

"The two realities seemed to blend together, between dream and reality. Suddenly the pale little boy turned around, smiling innocently and looked me right in the eyes."

Sarah and Jeshua's had horrified looks on their faces, even John visibly shook off a chill when Nick said this. It was starting to get obvious that Nick was having a hard time telling the story. The dream had obviously shaken him up and was shaking him up again as he recalled it for everyone.

"When the kid looked at me, I was suddenly filled with fear and wanted to run away as fast as I could, but for some reason I just sat there frozen in my tracks. It scared me so bad, because this kid's eyes were like black pools of vacant darkness. It's the only way I can describe it."

"Like I said, as soon as I'd seen his eyes, I was suddenly filled with panic. I felt a sudden urge to run, but I couldn't move. There was an overwhelming urge to keep looking, I simply couldn't turn away. Like something was holding me in place and making me look."

"The object on the child's lap, I still couldn't see it. Even though I was scared, I still needed to know what it was. When I willed myself to look and see what it was, I could only faintly make it out. It was some sort of glossy looking idol thing, but I wasn't sure."

"In my dream I suddenly realized I was no longer in the room and on the bed. I didn't know where I was. That was when I realized I was all a dream. Because before, I wasn't so sure."

They all nodded, confirming that they understood what

he was trying to explain.

"I was somewhere I'd never been before. Everything around me seemed to be hazy and dim. I knew I must be dreaming, but I had never had a dream like that before."

"This was so different from any other dream I'd ever had before or since then. I felt completely aware as if I was awake."

Everyone nodded, still listening intently as Nick continued telling about his dream.

"I looked around and tried to figure out where I was. That's when I could see a face emerging in the distance, directly ahead of me. It was slowly coming closer to me. The face, oddly enough, I somehow knew that it wasn't a real face."

'What was it?" asked Jeshua.

"I think it was a mask. Everything was hazy and seemed wrong. It was as if I didn't belong in that place at all. I knew I didn't belong there. Then I could see the face ahead of me more clearly."

"The mask?" Sarah asked.

"Yes, the mask or whatever it was. It seemed to look right at me. Something in my mind told me that it had seen me. Like it had looked directly at me and *in* me. Like, now that it had seen me, it knew me now. I can't really explain it."

"Wow, what happened after that?" Sarah asked.

"Nothing. The dream suddenly faded out after I seen the mask look at me. I woke up and everything was normal."

"It was a mask?" Jeshua asked.

"Yeah or like a mask. I never did see what the kid had, but I think it was the mask thing."

"What the kid had on the floor?" John asked.

"I couldn't see what it was. After he turned and looked at me with those dark eyes, the mask was now the only thing focused in my dream. I was somewhere else looking at the face or mask and the kid was gone. Everything was gone. Then I woke up."

Everyone went quiet for a moment as they took it all in.

"Wow, this is weird." Jeshua said. "You described her son perfectly and then you described exactly what he was doing on the floor when he was in our room in the middle of the night. What did the mask look like?"

"It sort of looked like a pumpkin or a squash. It was green and had this evil grin on it. It had black eyes that seemed to pierce right through you."

Jeshua visibly looked horrified at this point. He nearly had tears in his eyes when he said, "that kind of sounds like what his ceramic pencil holder looked like."

"Wow, really?" Nick said.

At this point, Nick wasn't sure if Jeshua was just pulling his leg or not. He knew what he dreamt that night years ago. He remembered it well. But after all, it was just a dream.

John got up from his seat and offered, "why don't you guys draw a picture of this thing and see if it's the same thing."

He motioned towards Nick and said, "you can draw the picture of the mask that was in your dream." Then he pointed towards Jeshua and said, "and you can draw a picture of the pencil holder your girlfriend's kid made."

They both agreed. After all, everyone was now very curious about the similarities.

John opened desk drawer and produced a few sheets of writing paper as well as a couple sharpened pencils. He handed the pencils and paper to Jeshua and Nick.

"Here, draw them out on separate ends of the room, so neither of you guys can see what the other one is drawing and then we'll see if what you guys are saying really matches up or not."

They both nodded in agreed and took the pencils and paper. Separating themselves in the room, Jeshua drew his picture on the top of John's glass display cabinet and Nick drew his on top a phone book that he placed on his lap.

Nick drew the picture of the mask he'd seen in his dream. Sarah noticed him getting slightly uncomfortable as he drew the details of the mask from his dream. She could tell that he really didn't want to recall it.

Nick finished his drawing and handed it to John.

John set it face down on the table without looking at it as everyone waited for Jeshua to finish his.

Jeshua noticed that Nick was already done and looked up at him.

"Wow, you're a fast drawer. I'm a little slower, give me a minute."

"Take all the time you need." John said.

A couple more minutes passed until Jeshua announced that he was done and handed his drawing to John. Everyone walked over to John, who set both drawings down on the glass cabinet so we could all see and compare the two side by side.

Jeshua's eyes widened when he compared the two. He immediately appeared stunned and frightened. Nick looked at the drawings as John picked them up and held them up to compare them even closer.

"They're the same," John announced after just a few seconds of studying them.

"I can't believe it! The mask in my dream and Jeshua's drawing of the ceramic pencil holder are the same."

"Yeah! Look both drawings have the same shape of heads, the same grins and the same round dark piercing eyes." Sarah said as she looked at the drawing with a stunned look on her face.

"It's scary, so say the least. If I hadn't seen it myself, I would have never believed it." John said.

John and Sarah were in disbelief.

"I don't know what to say. At first the two stories were just amusing, but now. Now, it's just plain scary. I don't think anyone really expected the two stories to really match up." John said.

"To be honest, I didn't either." Nick said.

"I especially didn't expect the two drawings would be exactly the same."

"This is now starting to scare me." Jeshua said.

"It's indeed very creepy." Sarah said.

"When did this happen," Nick asked. "When did you guys have this pencil holder thing?"

"Today. We've been unpacking boxes all day. We decided to take a break, so I came over here to visit for a little bit."

"Oh wow, do you still have it? I'd like to see it."

Everyone else in the room also agreed with Nick. They all wanted to see it now.

"I don't have it anymore."

"What happened to it?"

"She got so freaked out by it that she made me throw it away in the apartment's trash dumpster. I tossed it in the dumpster just before I headed here."

"If you threw it away this evening, then it should still be there." Sarah said.

"Yeah, you could go get it and show it to us. That way Nick can tell us if that's what he seen in his dream or not."

"I'm not really sure. I really don't want anything to do with it anymore. I tossed it in the dumpster. It's gone now."

"Well, you've already tried to get rid of it a couple of times," Sarah rationalized. "Throwing it in the dumpster probably isn't going to do it either. It's probably already back up in your apartment."

Jeshua began to turn pale and shuddered at the thought.

After thinking about it for a moment, he turned to Nick and asked, "would you like to go with me to find it? Please. I need someone to hold the flashlight for me and help me look. It's already starting to get dark outside."

After contemplating whether or not to go anywhere with a stranger, especially one that thought an art project made by a child was possessed or something. Against my better judgment, Nick agreed to go with him, but thought that Jeshua just wanted to make sure it wasn't back in his apartment.

Chapter 6

Nick left John and Sarah's apartment with Jeshua to help him recover this alleged horrifying object of Satan that he'd thrown away.

He really didn't take any of this too seriously. It was simply a recalled dream that he'd had which was strange and scary, but really nothing more than a dream. A dream that was fueled more by malnutrition and lack of sleep at the time than anything. Everything else was just a fluke coincidence. Plus, Nick really didn't think Jeshua was very stable and found him to be a bit of a religious fanatic.

Sure there were a lot of similarities, but really nothing more. Nevertheless, he really had nothing better to do that evening and the guy didn't' seem very big. So if he got weird, Nick knew that he could defend himself easily and take the guy down. So he was fairly confident he'd be safe enough to accompany him on this...witch hunt.

Jeshua drove a small red two seated MG convertible which he had the top down. It seemed like a toy car to Nick. They got in and Jeshua backed out of the parking lot and headed to the apartment complex Jeshua and his girlfriend had just moved into. This was here the dumpster in question was located so they could look for the pencil holder from hell. Nick really was amused someone would actually believe an inanimate object made by a small child would actually be possessed, or as Jeshua had put it, evil.

After a few minutes of driving on the highway, Nick's hair was severely wind blown hair. He really hated riding in convertibles and already regretted coming along.

Jeshua pulled into an apartment complex and steered his little convertible next to a large dumpster and parked.

"This is it." He announced. "This is where I threw it away."

Nick looked at the dumpster and instantly regretting coming even more than before. The dumpster was filthy and he didn't want to even get near it, much less touch it.

Nick nodded at him. "We may as well get this over with."

After turning off the car's engine, Jeshua got out of the car and approached the dumpster. Nick got out as well and followed behind him. There was some light radiating from the street light overhead, but not really that much. Nick looked at the trash dumpster. It was one of those tall ones that had siding doors on the sides. The sliding doors were open and he could see that it was half filled with garbage. Thankfully, most of the garbage appeared to be folded up discarded boxes.

He walked around to the other side, which wasn't lit by the street light very well and peered into the dumpster. He couldn't really see in it very well and wasn't sure if he was actually going to reach in and help look for the thrown away object.

"I'll look on that side with the flashlight and you can look on this side which is lit by the street light." Jeshua said, noticing Nick's apprehensiveness.

"Okay. But I'm telling ya right now, I'm not climbing in that nasty thing."

Jeshua didn't say anything as he went to his car and retrieved a flashlight then walked around to the other side of the dumpster and began searching through the rubbish inside. Nick watched him for a moment, until he bag looking through on his side that was partially lit up from the street light overhead.

The dumpster's sliding door was about waist high and he was able to shuffle through the boxes by just leaning over and not physically touching the dumpster. Nick didn't want its filth on him so he carefully pushed debris and boxes aside as he peered inside. He really had no idea what he was looking for and at this point he was only humoring Jeshua by looking.

Nick continued to rummage through the trash bin, pushing boxes to the side and looking inside the ones that were under them as he thought, "it's dark in here and I can hardly see anything, there is no way I am going to find something I didn't even know what looks like for certain."

At least he wasn't getting dirty. He was concerned about that when they arrived and seen the condition that the dumpster was in. The outside was filthy and he wasn't exactly motivated to dig through trash anyways.

Nick reached over to grab the bottom of a box to try to flip it over and look inside of it when suddenly something cold touched the back of his hand.

It was an icy cold touch that shot up his hand and went all the way up his arm within an instant. He didn't see what it was, but as soon as he felt it, he quickly withdrew his hand as fast as he could and jumped away from the trash dumpster with a yelp.

"Whoa!"

Startled, Nick just stood there and cradled his hand. His hand was now strangely cold to the touch, as if he'd had it in ice or something. The cold feeling sent a chilled feeling all through him. He'd never felt anything like that before.

Jeshua, whom was already about ready to give up looking, heard him cry out when he jumped away from the dumpster and quickly came around from the other side of the dumpster to make sure he was okay.

"Are you okay? What's the matter? Did you get cut or something?"

Embarrassed, Nick said "No, it was nothing. I touched something cold and it just spooked me for a second, that's all."

Jeshua walked up to where Nick had been looking in the dumpster and shined his flashlight inside.

After a moment of shining his flashlight around looking

inside the boxes, he leaned forward and reachined inside the dumpster.

"Here it is!"

Stepping back after retrieving it from the dumpster, he turned to face Nick and held it up to show him.

"Look, here it is."

He walked up to Nick and showed him his find in the light.

Nick looked at it and was instantly horrified.

"That's it! That's the face of the mask I'd seen in my dream...exactly!"

Nick couldn't believe it. It was definitely the face of the mask he'd seen in his dream. There was absolutely no denying it. It had the same deep green squash shaped head with its mouth agape and grinning. Even the black round glossy eyes that seemed to follow you as if they were actually looking at you. Its eyes seemed to pierce right through, as if it could see into your very soul. Its horrible mocking grin made it seem like it were an actual living object and laughing as it sensed your fear.

It felt like the air around them was thickening as the shadows seemed to darken as they gazed upon creepy object. Even the light from the street lamp seemed to dim slightly. Nick felt a cold wave shoot through his body and shuddered as he gazed upon the object in Jeshua's hands.

Jeshua noticed him shudder and said, "it scares the hell out of me too."

Nick simply nodded in agreement with saying a word.

Jeshua set it on the ground then walked towards his car.

"I'm going to wrap it in a t-shirt I have under my car seat."

After retrieving his t-shirt, he walked back and tossed the white t-shirt over the object.

"I don't like touching it." He said as he picked it up by the t-shirt and carefully wrapped the shirt around it. Satisfied it was wrapped well, he pulled out a "Holy Bible" that he had tucked under his arm and set the t-shirt wrapped object on top of it.

Nick didn't notice him grab the bible when he went to his car to fetch the t-shirt and didn't know he was carrying it under his arm. He just politely smiled thinking that it was a bit overkill, but made no comment about it. He knew how some religious fanatics were.

"I know I probably look silly putting it on a ninle, but I don't trust this thing. That's why I threw it away. I don't know why I let everyone talk me into coming back and fetching it."

Nick just smiled politely and nodded his head.

"We should probably head back."

"Yeah, I agree. My girlfriend's probably wondering why I'm taking so long. We were just taking a short break."

They got back into Jeshua's convertible and headed back to John and Sarah's apartment.

It was an even more uncomfortable ride heading back for Nick as he tried to ignore Jeshua repeating the Lord's Prayer over and over. Nick knew he was freaked out by the thing, but this was going a bit over the deep end.

He just sat quietly watching the scenery pass by as Jeshua drove them back.

Chapter 7

Nick and Jeshua arrived back at John and Sarah's apartment. After Jeshua parked his convertible Nick got out and quickly combed his hair back into place. He really didn't like riding in convertibles.

Jeshua retrieved the ceramic object that he still had wrapped in his t-shirt and again carried it on top of his bible. It was obvious that he was still afraid to touch it. Nick joined him as they walked up the entryway and knocked on the door. Sarah answered the door and welcomed them back in.

"Did you guys find what you were looking for?"

"Yes, we found it," Jeshua said as he held up his bible so she could see the wrapped bundle.

They walked into the room where they'd been before they left to go on their quest to find the accursed object from hell. Jeshua still held his bible up in front of him with the t-shirt wrapped object set on top of it. John was sitting on the couch reading a magazine when they came in. He put his reading aside and got up to greet them.

"Hey, welcome back. I see you managed to find it."

John and Sarah briefly gave at each other an equally mused look seeing Jeshua's superstitious fear of this thing when they seen how he was acting, carrying the thing on his bible and all.

"Bring the thing over here so I can see it under the lighting." John said as he walked over and flipped on the wall switch, turning on the overhead lights in the room.

He motioned for Jeshua to come over to where he was standing by the lamp on his display case.

Nick gave him some encouragement with a nudge from his elbow.

Nick walked across the room and stood next to John.

"Come on, bring it over there."

Jeshua followed Nick with Sarah in tow right behind him.

"Put it over here on the table." John said, pointing to the glass display case in the room.

Jeshua nodded and walked to the display case where John was standing. He was still holding the object on top of the bible in front of him as if it were some volatile dangerous object that would blow up at any moment.

As Jeshua started to carefully set the bible with the object down on the display case, John reached over and grabbed the object from on top of the bible and unwrapped the t-shirt from around it. Handing the t-shirt back to

Jeshua, he began to look it over, bringing it closer to his face to examine. A visible look of relief fell over on Jeshua's face, no longer having to carry the burden of his "evil object."

John flipped the ceramic object around in his hand as he continued examining it in the light.

Nick stood next to him looking over his shoulder trying to get a really good look at it himself. When Jeshua recovered it from the trash dumpster, Nick didn't really get a good look at it because Jeshua had wrapped it up right away and stuck it on his bible. That and the fact it was dark, he hadn't actually had a chance to see it up close and get a really good look at it.

Sarah stood behind Nick and was also looking at it as John was held it up examining it.

It didn't seem like there was anything really special about it. It was just a small ceramic object that fit into the palm of your hand. It was sculpted as a face and shaped somewhat like a gourd or small eggplant. It was glossy dark green.

The top of it was painted darker green, almost black, as if it was supposed to be hair or a horn or a combination of both. It had a pointed nose that hooked down like an old crone with a blackened mouth that was agape which had a small dark red tongue sticking out.

The eyes were painted black and beaming out of its sockets. The glossy eyes were as shiny as glass which made them seem to follow you wherever you moved. It was a bit strange and undeniably creepy, but innocently enough, you could tell it was made by a child. No matter how creepy looking it was.

"It doesn't really look scary." Nick said.

John nodded in agreement. Sarah said nothing and just continued to look at it.

"Sure it's a bit creepy looking, but maybe he was trying to make it look like a monster or something."

"Yeah, I think so too." John said.

Nick looked at it as John held it in front of him and pointed at its eyes.

"See, he even has the eyes bulging out and everything to make it look sort of evil."

Jeshua was unconvinced and looked away slightly shaking his head.

Sarah took it from John's hands to look at it more closely.

"It's not very heavy," she remarked as she held it in one hand as if comparing its weight.

She handed it to Nick and asked Jeshua, "you say he said that it's a pencil holder?"

Nick examined it closely while he held it.

Jeshua, who had been standing back away from the object while watching us, straightened up.

"Yes, he said it was a pencil holder. He made it in art

class for his Mom."

Nick continued to inspected it with greater scrutiny. It weighed no more than that of a rock of similar size. Perhaps a little lighter than a rock. There were a few small holes around its face where it could a hold a pencil if one were inserted into one of the holes. It had a total eight pencil holes going around its sides.

Still examining it, Nick observed, "it's really more of a paper weight than a pencil holder."

John agreed.

"It felt cold to me when I held it. Did it feel cold to you , John?"

"Eh, it's probably from being outside, it's starting to get a little chilly outside," John said as he shrugged his shoulders.

Nick agreed, thinking nothing more of the object's coldness. He wasn't about to mention how its coldness spooked him when he accidentally touched it in the dumpster.

Nick walked over to Jeshua and handed it to him saying, "I don't think there's anything to it. It's just a creepy paper weight made of ceramic."

Seeing Nick try to hand it to him, Jeshua stepped back and held his hands up.

"Whoa no way man, I don't want that thing. Don't give it to me."

As soon as he said that, everyone chucked at his expense.

With a raised eyebrow, Nick asked him, "you're not scared of it are you? It's just a ceramic paper weight."

Jeshua looked a little embarrassed now.

"Nope, I want nothing to do with it. I know y'all think I'm crazy, but I really just wanted to make sure it didn't find its way back into our apartment."

Nick shrugged his shoulders and held the object up to everyone.

"Does anyone want it?"

Everyone in the room shook their heads 'no.'

With nobody wanting it, he walked across the room where a small trash basket was and went to throw it away.

Sarah quickly stopped him and said, "don't throw it in there. I don't want that thing in my house."

"I thought you said it wasn't cursed."

She giggled nervously and said, "yeah, but by the way y'all's stories matched up, it's just way too creepy for me."

Nick laughed and laid it on his jacket that he'd set on the love seat when we came in.

"I'll just take it with me and toss it in the dumpster when I pass it on my way home."

Sarah nodded, obviously relieved.

John amused by it all, just shook his head in

bewilderment and said nothing, unable to hide his grin.

Before Sarah could say anything to him, the phone rang in the other room. She gave John a look and got up from the couch where she'd just sat down and left to answer the telephone in the other room.

"Well, I've stayed a bit longer than I was supposed to and Connie is probably waiting for me to get home and help her finish unpacking. Tell Sarah bye for me. I have to go."

Jeshua shook Nick's hand and said, "it was nice meeting you and thanks for humoring me by going out and getting that... thing."

"It was nice meeting you." Nick lied, he thought Jeshua was pretty strange and was glad he was leaving.

He then shook John's hand and called out to Sarah, whom was still on the phone, "I'll call y'all tomorrow" as he departed out the front door.

John closed the door behind him and returned to the room they were in.

"Well, that was an odd visit if I don't say so myself."

Nick laughed.

"Yeah, I think he's hit the bible a bit too hard and is seeing demons in everything."

This made John laugh loudly.

"For a minute there, I thought he was going to perform an exorcism on it."

They both burst out in laughter just as Sarah came back to the room.

"What are you guys laughing about?"

John shook his head and said, "oh nothing, we were just joking about your cousin and the demon pencil holder."

Hearing John refer to it as a 'demon pencil holder' made them start laughing again.

"You guys are mean." Sarah said, starting to laugh herself.

Nick fetched his jacket from the love seat and put it on. He took the ceramic object and placed it in his jacket pocket and said, "I'll just take this with me and toss it in the dumpster on my way home."

Sarah held a hand up and said, "don't throw it away yet."

"Why not?"

"That was Laura on the phone. I told her about it and she wants to see it herself."

Nick nodded and rolled his eyes.

"She wanted to know if you'd stop by and show it to her. I already told her you would," she added while smiling.

John laughed under his breath.

Sarah down on the couch next to John and in a slightly higher tone, "she also said that she's cooking spaghetti if you want to come over and have some."

Nick looked up at Sarah and smiled. It seemed his secret crush on Laura was obvious to everyone.

John scratched the side of his scruffy beard and said, "yeah, he wants...spaghetti." He grinned and gave Sarah a look.

Sarah immediately swatted John on the arm, shushing him.

On that note Nick figured it was best to go.

"Okay, well...I'll stop by and show her the demon paper weight."

They all had another laugh at it being referenced as a 'demon paper weight.'

They continued to laugh about it as Nick headed to the front door then said while opening it, "thanks, I'll see you guys later!"

In unison, John and Sarah replied "see ya later," waving 'good-bye' as he stepped out the door, shutting it behind him.

Nick stepped onto the sidewalk and noticed Jeshua sitting in his car in the parking lot. He tried to avoid him by walking to the side, but Jeshua noticed him and waved.

"Hey! Come here a second."

Nick paused a second hesitantly, but then walked over to Jeshua's car.

"What's up?"

"Hey, I know I just met you and all, and you don't me very well. But would you like to come over and drink some whiskey?"

His advance made Nick very uncomfortable. Even a little bit angry, but he kept it to himself and remained polite.

"No thanks, man. I appreciate the offer, but I gotta go. See ya."

Nick waved as he walked off then turned onto the sidewalk and began making his way through the apartment complex's maze of poorly lit and dimly covered walkways.

Walking through the apartment complex with its turns around dark corners, Nick weaved his way towards Steve's apartment where Steve and Laura were apparently waiting for him.

Nick really didn't understand why they didn't light this place up any better as he made his way through unlit passageways and paths. If anything, he figured they'd at last have it lit for safety and security reasons so they wouldn't get sued for liability.

Nick felt a chill from the wind hit him as he walked along the labyrinthine sidewalks. The cold breeze sent a chill all the way down his neck and trickled into his spine. It made him shudder.

As he continued walking, Nick noticed the weight of the object in his pocket. It felt heavy than it should be and made him feel very uncomfortable. In fact, the weight of it seemed more than it previously had been. Before when he was examining it at John and Sarah's, it seemed lighter than a rock of similar size. Much like anything else made of ceramic. But now it seemed heavier as if it were made of lead or some other heavy metal. He tried to ignore it.

Nick zigzagged through a memorized pattern within the apartment complex and quickened his pace as he walked. He couldn't help the feeling of being watched from the shadows.

He felt like eyes were on him at every dark corner he approached. The feeling was overwhelming, even though he knew it was ridiculous. He knew nothing was in the shadows following or watching him. It was just that guy's superstition over the object had him on edge. It gave him the "eeby-jeebies."

Even though he knew it was his imagination, he wasn't able to shake the overwhelming feeling of dread creeping up on him. It felt like something was closing in on him. It seemed like someone or something was just around every darkened corner he passed about to lunge out at him in ambush as I walked by.

He kept looking over his shoulder to make sure nothing was behind him. It felt like someone was behind him, stalking.

The shadows grew darker and slowly reached towards him. His heart gradually start racing in the growing anxiety. He kept walking at a quickened pace, rushing to reach his destination.

He stepped off the sidewalk and walked across the parking lot towards the final complex's matrix and stepped up over the curb onto the sidewalk. Walking along the darkened sidewalk and turned the final corner to reach Steve's apartment. When he passed the final dark corner, he heard a scuffling behind him.

Nick turned to look, but the wind picked up and prevented him from being able to tell where the sound came from. The wind blew right through him and chilled him to the bone, making his whole body shiver.

Nick turned back around and quickened his pace to an almost jog as he darted around the corner and headed straight towards Steve's apartment door. As he reached the entryway, he nervously over his shoulder to see if anything was following him, but only seen darkness.

Nick knocked on the door, trying not to appear nervous because he noticed himself getting visibly panicked and jumpy. The wind picked up again and he heard the leaves blowing in the trees around him.

Something was out there.

He could feel its eyes on him. Peering at him from its hiding place in the darkness. The shadows crept up from around the corner stretching towards him as he stood there alone. The wind's chill made goosebumps form on his arms, along with the feeling that something he couldn't see was approaching him. He fought the urge to run as his heart rate began to race.

Nick looked around in the darkness behind him.

Searching the shadows, hoping to see what was may or may not be there. He turned towards the door and reached up to knock on it again when suddenly the porch light buzzed loudly and popped in an explosion of white light.

He stood there stunned by the sudden bright flash of light that temporarily blinded him and left him vulnerable in total darkness. As he rubbed his eyes and began to feel cold hands touching his legs.

Something behind him was touching his legs and he couldn't see what it was. It felt like small child-like hands, several of them and they were cold as ice as they touched his legs. He tried blinking his eyes to see what it was, but was unable to see as he tried waving his hands by his legs to feel whatever was touching him.

When he tried to feel what was touching his legs, he felt something breathe its cold, icy breath down the back of his neck. Its cold angry breath panted its hatred on him and squeezed the warm air right out of him. It made his own breath cold and choked him, making it hard for him to breathe.

Even though he still couldn't see, Nick started to turn around in order to try to get away and flee the cold blackness that was engulfing him.

Just when he was about to take flight to escape, light bathed him, rescuing him from the darkness. He was now able to see around him.

The apartment door had suddenly opened as Laura answered the door. When she opened the door, it lit up everything around him with the light from inside the apartment.

Still startled, Nick was frantically looking around him to see whatever it was that had just attacked him. He saw nothing.

Seeing him looking around with a wild look in his eyes, Laura asked him, "are you okay?"

He turned and looked at her, now aware of how shaken he must look and said, "yeah, I'm fine."

Now a little embarrassed, he smiled at her and said, "your porch light blew out and it startled me for a second, that's all."

She looked around the doorway at the porch light and seen that it was out. She tried flicking the wall switch off and on attempting to get it to turn back on.

Unsuccessful, she turned and hollered behind her, "Steve! The porch light blew out!"

Nick heard the familiar voice of Steve replying back to her saying, "okay! I'll see if I have any more light bulbs in the cabinet."

Laura stepped aside, smiling at Nick and said, "please come in."

Nick stepped inside the apartment and seen Steve across the hallway in the dining room. He was fiddling with his broken stereo amplifier that he had in several disassembled pieces along the top of the dining room table.

Without even being told, Nick knew that Steve had probably blown it earlier when he was cranking the stereo's volume too loud. It was his first and most probable guess. Nick was more surprised Steve didn't shatter the patio window in the living room from the vibrations coming off the bass speakers.

The apartment and city noise ordinances weren't in effect between the hours of 10 a.m. through 8 p.m. and Steve took full advantage of that fact with a stereo system that encompassed nearly half the wall in his living room area.

His apartment was surrounded by five foot speakers which he had wired throughout the place on all floors of the two-story townhouse apartment. The Speakers had woofers that would make your heart skip a beat or three if you stood too close to one of them while the system was turned up loud.

They'd often joked about how they would all probably go deaf before they reached middle age. However they didn't care, life was too short to worry about such trifles. After all, what's life if you have never lived.

"Hey Steve!" Nick said as he took off his jacket.

"Hey man! Come over here and check this out."

Nick walked down the hallway towards the dining room, holding his jacket over his arm.

Laura followed behind him and asked, "did you bring that weird thing with you?"

Nick turned his head towards her and smiled as he continued walking down the hallway towards the dining room.

When she caught up beside him, he held up his jacket and said, "I have it right here." As they reached the dining room.

"Hey, how's it going?" Nick asked Steve.

"Hey man, not much."

Steve was looking down at the assorted electronics across the table that was once his stereo amplifier.

"I'm just trying to see if I can fix this thing."

"What happened? It was working earlier today."

"I think it may have overheated or something. I've been testing the circuits and they all seem fine."

Nick reached into his jacket pocket and took the ceramic object out. Immediately he noticed that it felt icy cold in his hand.

"Ooo, let me see it." Laura beamed.

Nick hesitated handing it to her, the coldness he felt from it had ran up his arm. It made goosebumps start to form and even made the hairs on the back of his neck stand on end. This thing gave me the creeps.

Laura ignored his hesitation and took the object from his hand.

"Oh weird, it feels cold."

She turned towards Steve and said, "check this out, it's icy cold."

Steve was preoccupied with his electronics and didn't look up.

"Steve, touch it. It's weird. It feels cold."

Steve looked up at her oddly and then in order to humor her so he could go back to his repair work, reached over and touched it.

Steve let out a yelped the moment he touched it and quickly withdraw his hand.

Laura laughed as soon as he pulled his hand back. He frowned his eyebrows at Laura and then looked at Nick with a questioning look on his face.

"How did you do that? That's weird."

He looked at Laura and then back at Nick again. "how did you get it cold like that?"

Steve reached over and touched it again.

"It's weird, huh?" Laura said.

She felt the top of it as Steve did, holding the object in her other hand.

As they were examining it, Nick hung his jacket on the back of one of the dining room chairs. He sat down in the chair and began telling them about the weird guy, Jeshua, that came over to John and Sarah's apartment and how they'd drawn matching pictures of this thing. He told them about the kid he'd dreamt about years ago and it matched the kid's description that made the ceramic object in art class.

Steve and Laura seemed interested as he continued on about how they went to Jeshua's apartment dumpster to retrieve it and how he acted when they found it. He mentioned how the guy had wrapped it up in a t-shirt and placed it on a bible while he recited the Lord's Prayer all the way back to John and Sarah's apartment.

They both got a kick out of that and laughed about it.

Laura set it on the table and said, "well, it looks creepy enough."

"Yeah. It's definitely a creepy thing, especially how you had a dream about it before even seeing or meeting this guy." Steve said.

"I had that dream a few years ago and besides the pencil holes on its sides, it does look exactly like the mask in my dream."

Laura visibly shuddered when Nick pointed that out.

Steve smiled as he looked at Laura and said, "what's the matter, someone walk over your grave?"

She looked back at him and smiled. "Yeah, it felt like it. It sent chills down my back. How creepy."

Suddenly all three of them jumped from fright when a loud screech hissed in the kitchen.

In unison, they look into the kitchen and see a pot on top of the electric range was boiling over the sides.

Laura was boiling spaghetti noodles and the water had boiled over. It was foaming over the pot and landing on the red hot electric burner which made a loud hissing sound as the liquid hit the burner.

Realizing what it had spooked them, they laughed at our own expense.

Laura quickly got up from her chair and rushed into the kitchen to tend to the pot boiling over by removing it from the heat and shutting off the burner.

"Jeez, this whole thing's made us jumpy and easy to scare."

"It's just too weird. There are too many creepy and unexplainable coincidences."

"Yeah, it's made us a bit jumpy. The water hitting the burner and hissing was simply perfect timing."

Laura grabbed a large wooden spoon that had been setting on the counter and stirred the noodles.

"The noodles are done."

She lifted the pot and poured the spaghetti noodles into an awaiting colander that she had setting in the sink. Letting the noodles drain, she placed the empty scorching hot stainless steel pot on top of a pot holder on the counter and returned to the dining room.

"Are you going to stay for dinner? There's plenty. In fact, I think I made too much." She asked Nick.

Nick looked up at the clock that hanging on the wall. It

was nine forty-three, almost ten o' clock. He had to be home before ten and he couldn't be late.

He got up from the chair and said, "no thanks, I have to get home."

"Are you sure?"

"Yeah. I appreciate it and wish I could stay, but it's my ass if I'm late."

He lifted his jacket off the back of the chair and put it on.

"Good luck with the stereo man, I hope you get it back in action." He said as he started walking towards the door.

Sporting a coy smirk, Steve looked up and said, "yeah, me too. I think it just overheated and probably work as soon as I plug it back in. I'll catch ya later."

Nick turned towards Laura, whom was in the kitchen and stealthily looked upon her while she was turned away busying herself with their dinner. She was wearing tight jeans that formed and shaped over her body, bobbi socks, and a yellow blouse tucked into her pants. Nick could see her bra through her blouse which drew a slight involuntary smile on his lips. He couldn't help looking at her.

When he looked back up, she was looking right back at him. Nick knew she'd seen him undressing her with his eyes and was smiling back at him mischievously.

Embarrassed, he turned away and started walking down the hallway towards the door while saying, "I'll catch y'all later"

118

Laura quickly stepped out of the kitchen and said, "wait a second, aren't you going to take that thing with you?"

Nick turned and looked at her with a half cocked smile. She pointed at the ceramic object setting on the table that he'd brought over.

Smiling as he looked at it and said, "you don't want it?" He knew she didn't, but he couldn't help teasing her.

"To be honest. I was actually going to toss it in the dumpster on my way here."

Still looking down at his electrical work and holding the probes of a multimeter, Steve said "just toss it in the trash over there." He motioned towards the small kitchen trash can next to the wall.

"Okay," Nick replied with a shrug as he reached over to picked up and tossed it in the trash can.

Laura just stood there motionless with her head cocked to the side and slightly jaw dropped. It was obvious it made her feel really uneasy and she didn't want it there. Not even in the trash can.

"No way, I don't want it here."

"What? Why?"

"Because. It's creepy."

"You don't actually think it's possessed, do you?"

"No, but still."

"It's okay. I'll toss it in the dumpster when I take the

trash out."

"When are you taking the trash out?"

"After I eat. Don't worry."

"Fine."

Nick stood there for a minute feeling guilty that the object he'd brought over had caused a small argument between Stave and Laura.

Seeing the look on her face, Nick smiled knowingly at her and stepped back into the dining room to retrieve it.

"I'll just toss it in the dumpster on my way home. It's no problem."

Steve abruptly got up and grabbed it off the table and tossed it into the kitchen trash can.

"No worries dude. I'll carry the trash out after dinner."

Not wanting to get into the middle of whatever argument they were having and able to tell that Steve was agitated by something, Nick wisely decided to say nothing.

"Alright man, I'll see ya later." Nick said and turned to leave.

"I'll walk him out so I can lock the door behind him." She said to Steve.

Steve just nodded without looking up, busy putting his amplifier back together.

Laura walked quickly and caught up to Nick whom was already at the door.

Nick reached down to grab the knob to open the door and Laura reached down at the same time and covered his hand over the door knob. He looked up a her and she smiled at him while gently squeezing his hand.

Nick smiled back at her, not quite sure what to think or do. She released his hand and low seductive voice, "I'll see you later."

Shyly he looked away and turned the door knob, opening the door. She still held her gaze as he opened the door and then 'accidentally' brushed the back of her hand along my outer thigh as she to pull the door open.

Nick's nervously smiled again and she stepped back and opened the door the rest of the way.

Nick looked away and stepped outside.

He turned back towards her and said "I'll see ya later."

She just smiled at him and held a seductive gaze at him. He wasn't sure what to think about that at all. All kinds of thoughts and uncertainties ran through his head.

Nick waved as Laura slowly closed the door and watched him walk away. He shyly turned to look back as he was walking and seen that she was looking at his backside. Her eyes lifted and met his as she bite the bottom of her lip and then shut the door the rest of the way.

Nick was stunned. He knew that Steve probably hadn't said anything to her yet. Although he was acting rather cold towards her. But Nick just figured it was because he was busy working on his amplifier trying to get it to work.

Maybe he did say something to her.

His thoughts were suddenly stopped when he realized that the porch light was on. The one that blew out with a loud pop and flask. It hadn't been changed yet and it was on.

He turned to look back and look at the porch light and just as he did, it blinked out.

Instantly he remembered what had happened when he arrived stood there in the darkness. He turned and quickly walked home trying to rationalize it away.

Perhaps she did change it and he didn't notice or maybe it didn't burn out and just shorted or something. She'd probably turned it out after closing the door and figuring that he'd walked away far enough and didn't need it.

Chapter 8

Nick woke up the next morning to the sound of metal banging outside. It was the garbage truck emptying the apartment's dumpsters that were spread throughout the complex.

The dumpster lids banged loudly as they slammed down against the metal sides when the garbage truck lifted it over its top and dumped the contents inside its cargo hold area. Then lids would slam down again when the dumpster was set back down. This was in addition to the already loud truck revving its engine to run its hydraulics to lift the dumpster. If that didn't get your attention, then the high pitched beeping it made when it backed up definitely would.

'Well, that's the end of that thing. That is, if Steve remembered to take the trash out.'

The dumpster's contents would soon be taken to the dump and would be gone forever in the decay of society's discarded disgust and waste. The creepy object was now forever gone, never to be recovered no matter how badly anyone would want to.

It was just as well that Nick was awakened by the garbage truck. It was almost time for him to get up for work anyways. He was suppose to show up at 6:30 a.m. to meet with the rest of the roofing crew.

The roof they were working was only a couple of buildings down the road. With the entire roofing crew also living in the apartment complex, everyone getting to work was never a problem. Only half the time did Kenneth's or Nick's dad actually show up at the job site to tell them what to do. It was usually Tom, Kenneth's uncle, that told them what to do and got them started for work.

They usually only worked for about six hours at most and quit about the time the Oklahoma Sun made the black top roofs just too unbearably hot to work on any further. That was when they'd quit for the day. It was a no brainer.

Nick sat up in bed, staring blankly at nothing. He heard sirens outside down the street.

'May as well get it over with as there was no getting out of it.'

He got up out of bed and got dressed for work. As he headed out the door, he noticed that his dad wasn't home and had already left.

'Great, he's going to be on the job site bitching at us all day.'

Nick began to walk towards the job site. He noticed the garbage collection truck was parked next to a dumpster. There was also a couple police cars there as well.

"I've never seen a garbage truck get a ticket before." he

After a short walk, Nick arrived on the job site. He noticed that Kenneth, David, and Tom were already at the side of the building and working. It was unusual for them to beat Nick to there. They were usually the stragglers that were the last ones on the job site. They even had the extension ladder already up to the roof and were getting the tools ready to be hauled up via rope tied to a bucket method. David was up on the roof holding the rope with Kenneth below filling the bucket full of tools.

Nick walked over to Kenneth and helped him finish loading the tools in the bucket.

"Hey, did you see the cops over there?" asked Kenneth.

"Yeah. Are they giving the garbage truck driver a ticket?"

"I don't know. The garbage truck was already parked there when we got here. He was leaning out of his door looking in the dumpster."

"Maybe he found something in it."

"Who knows....or cares."

After they filled the bucket, they stepped back and signaled David to pull it up. As David pulled the tools up, Kenneth and Nick walked around to climb up the ladder and get on the roof.

As Nick stood and held the ladder steady while Kenneth went up, Tom walked up behind him and tapped him on the shoulder with a pair of leather gloves.

"You left these on the roof again yesterday."

"Thanks."

"Your dad was pissed off. He started bitching about tools being left out and everything being done half-assed"

He walked past Nick and stood at the foot of the ladder and said, "he told me to give those to you and to tell you to get your head out of your ass."

Tom giggled after making that remark and started to climb up the ladder and said as went up, "get your head out of your ass, those were his exact words."

It definitely sounded like his dad, Nick had no doubt those were his exact words.

Nick took his gloves and put them on before he climbed up the ladder to get on the roof and start working. It was going to be another hot day and they knew to work as fast as they could to get the roof done before the scorching heat set in.

Nick walked over to the other end of the roof where David had set the tools. Kenneth was already over there standing over the tools.

Tom told them to start working on the opposite corner of the roof. Nick stepped beside him and bent down to pick up one of the brooms. He wanted to sweep the roof one last time before they got started to make sure the new roofing adhered well to the surface. If they didn't do this and some of the roof bubbled or came up from dirt underneath, it was guaranteed that they'd hear about it.

For an unwilling work crew, they were pretty efficient.

As Nick bent down to grab the broom, the wind picked up and blew his hat off his head. His hat blew right over the side of the building. Annoyed, he cussed under his breath and looked over the side of the building to see where it landed.

Kenneth, who was still standing next to him, seen it happen and started laughing. He stepped over next to Nick and looked over the side of the building, still laughing about it. This just irritated Nick even more.

Nick spotted his hat drifting in the wind until it landed halfway across the parking lot towards the field behind the apartment complex.

"Dude, there it goes" Kenneth said, laughing at Nick.

"Man, that sucks."

Nick headed towards the ladder to go down and fetch his hat before someone drove by and ran it over. With the day's heat on the roof, he would need his hat or he'd cook under the hot sun.

Kenneth was still laughing and pointed at it, saying "there it goes again."

Nick looked over to where his hat had blown on the road just in time to see the wind pick it up again and blow it across the road. He cursed under his breath as it tumbled into the field until it finally settled at the base of small weed bush.

He removed his gloves and tossed them on the roof next

to the ladder,

"Tom, I'll be right back! My hat blew off my head. I'm going to go fetch it real quick!"

"Hurry up! Your dad's suppose to stop by. I'll be damned if I get in trouble because you're messing around."

"I'll be quick."

Nick quickly scurried down the ladder and jogged across the road to retrieve his hat. He started walking through grassy field where his hat had blown when noticed his work boots were getting wet. Looking down, he seen that tall grass was covered in morning dew. He hoped that his hat didn't get soaking wet from it.

He walked the rest of the way through the wet grass to where his hat rested against a patch of brush. He still couldn't believe that his hat had blown off the roof and then blew all the way across the field. When he bent down to pick it up, as soon as he lifted his hat up from the ground, he noticed something in the grass under his hat in the grass.

Nick bent down closer to get a better look, pushing the wet grass aside to see what it was.

It was that ceramic object!

There it was with it's mocking smile and beady eyes staring back at him!

Even worse was that it was on the ground right under where his hat had blown. What were the chances? There was no way it could be the same creepy ceramic object from yesterday that Steve threw in the garbage can. Threw away in the garbage that supposedly was thrown into the dumpster and emptied by collectors this morning.

Nick knew Steve threw it in the garbage can last night and as far as he knew Steve had thrown his garbage in the dumpster. Steve was a bit obsessive-compulsive about taking the trash out. Nick knew him well enough to know that he didn't go to bed until he'd taken the trash out to the dumpster every night. He also knew that the garbage collectors had been there early this morning to empty the dumpsters as well. It was what woke him up this morning.

There was no way that it could be right there laying in the grass. But there it was.

Nick felt chills go through him as he considered what Jeshua had said about it reappearing whenever he tried to get rid of it. He was starting to think that it was no coincidence that his hat just simply blew off and landed exactly where this thing was in the field. This object was supposed to be gone forever. It was supposed to be rotting in the dump's decay with the rest of the dumpster garbage that had been carried off this morning.

'Why was it here on the ground in this grassy field. Did Steve really throw it there?'

Nick stood up and inspected his hat to make sure it wasn't wet and brushed off a little dirt from it before putting it back on. He then bent back down to look at the object in the grass a little closer. He seriously doubted that this was the same object from yesterday. Maybe his eyes were just playing tricks on him. Or maybe Steve didn't really throw it away in the dumpster with the rest of his trash like he said he would. Maybe Steve took it out of the trash last night and chucked it into the field last night.

That would be the only real explanation, Nick reasoned. There was no way that this thing could have just simply appeared out of nowhere. It made a lot more sense that Steve must have thrown it into the field, either last night or early this morning. It was just pure dumb luck that his hat happened to blow off his head and landed exactly where the object was in the field.

That really was the only feasible explanation. To think otherwise was simply ludicrous and Nick wasn't going to be suckered into it.

He reached down to pick it up so he look at it closer.

"Nick!!"

As soon as his hand touched it he heard his name called out behind him.

"Nick! What the fuck are you doing over there!?"

Nick turned to look in the direction of the yelling and seen his dad standing by the ladders looking at him.

His dad looked angry.

"Why aren't you on the roof working?!" He heard his dad yell out.

Nick quickly stood up and started walking back towards the work site in a haft trot.

"I walk around the corner and the first thing I see is you fucking around over there. I don't pay you to mess around,

I pay you to work on that roof.'

Nick knew not to respond, it would only further fuel his dad's anger and make things worse.

"Don't bother getting back on the roof, you're fired. I'll find someone else that actually wants to work and not fuck around on the job."

With that he turned around and walked away, still cussing under his breath. The guys on the roof, seeing Nick get chewed out and then get fired on the spot, were scrambling look busy so they wouldn't get fired too.

Stunned, Nick just stood there for a moment as he watched his dad angrily march off.

He continued to stand there as he watched him walk around the corner and out of sight. Glancing up on the roof, they guys pretended not to see him.

Nick took it all in. Even though he didn't even want to work for his dad on the roofs anyways, this was not how he wanted to end it. Not with his dad angry and firing him. He'd hoped to end it by finishing the roofs on contract. Plus, Tom could have grabbed his balls and defended him by letting his dad know that he was just fetching his hat and that he'd said it was okay for him to go get it.

Nick looked up on the roof and seen Tom with his back to him, avoiding eye contact.

"What a Coward." Nick said under his breath.

He wasn't going to let this bother him. This was actually a golden opportunity to go out and find a job that didn't involve manual labor or the blistering heat.

Nick walked back to where the object was in the grass and looked down at it. After a moment of reflecting how things quickly went down hill, he bent down and picked it up. As usual it felt cold to the touch, but it also had been in the morning dew which was probably why it felt colder than it should have been. He momentarily inspected it before stuffing it in his back pocket and began walking back home. He wasn't going to let any of this bother him. He was going to change out from his work clothes and go look for another job. It was as simple as that.

While Nick walked home he heard his name called out as he passed by Steve's apartment. It was Laura. She was standing in the doorway of Steve's apartment and waving at him to get his attention. Nick instantly warmed up and walked towards her.

"I thought you had to work today?"

He nodded his head and smiled as

"I did have to work today, but I just got fired."

"What? Why?"

Eh, it's nothing. I was on the roof starting work and my hat blew off, so I got off the roof to go fetch it. When I went to get it, my dad showed up and fired me for not working."

"What? That's a bit harsh."

"It's no big deal. I hated working of those roofs anyways."

"Still, that was a bit petty."

"He's a bit of a hot head, always has been. I was surprised to get fired, but at the same time it was no surprise, if you know what I mean."

"Sure. Hey, did you hear the police found a body in the dumpster?"

"What?"

"Yeah. The one over there." she pointed to one of the dumpsters on the road.

"Wow. was that why the police were here earlier?"

"Yeah, Steve went and looked when they pulled it out of the dumpster. He said the guy's eyes were blackened out."

"Seriously?"

"He said it was freaky looking."

"That's weird as hell. This whole day has been weird."

"What do you mean?"

"My hat blew off the roof when I was at work earlier and landed in that field."

Nick pointed to the field. Laura nodded her head, listening.

"I can see that being a little weird, landing that far away."

"Oh not really, we're a couple stories up on the roof. A good gust of wind can carry it even further than that. The weird part is, it landed on this in the field."

Nick reached into his pocket, pulled out the ceramic object and showed it to her. She took a step back and her eyes grew big soon as she seen him pull it out and show it to her.

"My hat landed right on top of this thing when it landed in the field over there."

"Oh my god, that's the thing Steve threw away in the dumpster last night," she said as she turned inside the apartment's and called for Steve to come out.

"Steve! Come here!"

She turned and looked at it again in disbelief.

"Steve, come here a minute! Nick has that thing again!"

Steve walked over to the door. He appeared groggy, as if he'd just got out of bed.

"Hey man, How's it going?

"Not bad."

"I thought you had to work today."

"Look what Nick has." Laura interrupted. "Look, it's that the thing you threw away in the dumpster last night."

Steve looked at the object Nick was holding with a disinterested look on his face.

'Yeah, I tossed that thing in the dumpster last night with the rest of our trash. What did you do, go digging in the dumpster for it?"

"No, I found it in that field over there." Nick pointed

136

towards the field.

"What? What was it doing out there?"

"I have no idea. I found it by chance when I had to go fetch my hat."

"Your hat? What was you hat doing in the field?"

"I was up on the roof and it blew off my head and landed over there."

Steve nodded.

"When I went to grab it, this was under it."

He smiled and gave Nick a look that showed that he didn't believe him.

"No way. You had to go and dig it out of the trash dumpster. There is no way that thing was in the field this morning. I threw it away last night."

Nick shook his head, denying it.

"I even remember picking it up out of the trash to look at it for second just before I carried everything out to the dumpster."

Nick raised an eyebrow.

"Seriously dude, I tossed it back in the garbage bag and sealed it up last night before I carried it out and threw it in the dumpster."

Laura shook her head, confirming everything Steve said.

Nick looked towards the empty dumpster across the parking lot and then looked at Steve inquisitively.

"I don't know, because I know I didn't go digging in the trash."

"It's definitely weird." Laura said.

"It's probably someone just messing with us is all."

Steve replied with a loud "Ha! You're the one trying messing with us. You grabbed that thing out of the trash last night or this morning to try to fool us. Because I threw that thing away and I know it was in the dumpster last night."

"Nope, it wasn't me. I didn't get it out. I woke up to the garbage truck emptying it this morning. I didn't get the chance to dig it out, even if I wanted to."

"Yeah, sure dude. I believe you." Steve said rolling his eyes.

 Steve stepped inside the apartment and disappeared around the corner for a moment.

"I'm serous, I didn't go dig it out. Maybe he threw it in the field or something."

"I believe you." Laura said, trying to reassure Nick.

Steve appeared back in the doorway.

"Well, I must head off to work anyways. I'll catch y'all later." He said as he walked out the door past Laura.

He briefly stopped in front of Nick and said, "Nice try but I'm not fooled by your 'cursed' object."

Nick just smiled. He wasn't so sure that Steve threw it

in the dumpster and thought he'd thrown it in the field and just wasn't admitting it. Even still, what were the chances that his hat would land on it and he'd find it. It was in a field of tall grass. The chances of ever running across it ever again were slim to nothing. It was the first time Nick had even walked in that field.

"I have to go, I will see ya later." Steve said as he walked off towards his parked car.

They watched Steve drove off then Nick turned to Laura and said, "well, I'm going to find a way to smash this thing and destroy it forever. I'm not sure if Steve threw it in the field or someone else did. But either way, I'm making it disappear for real this time."

"Yeah, you should smash it. I don't like that thing at all."

Nick nodded his head in agreement.

"I have to find a safe place to smash it. I don't want to smash it on the road or anything like that and then have a million pieces scattered everywhere that I'll have to clean up."

Laura laughed. "Nope, you don't want a huge mess to clean up."

"Hmm, I wonder where I could smash it. Maybe I could throw it hard against the inside of the dumpster."

"Even better, you could use the concrete wall at the creek over there to smash it."

She pointed towards the creek across the street from where they were standing. Nick looked over to where she was pointing and seen the creek's concrete support wall and smiled.

"Yeah, that would be a good place to smash it.

Nick turned back and looked at Laura and smile.

"I'm going to go over there and smash it. I'll see ya later."

"Yeah, I have to get ready for the day. Good luck."

Nick stuck the object back in his pocket and waved goodbye as he parted while Laura went back inside, shutting the door behind her.

He walked across the road and across part of the grassy field to where the creek was located.

There was a grassy slope that led down to the creek bed. Nick carefully walked down, being mindful not to slip on the wet dew covered grass. The last thing he wanted to do was tumble down the slope into the creek's mud.

The creek's support wall, which was on the opposite side of where Nick stood, was made of reinforced concrete and stood about twenty feet high. The wall ran along the creek for about forty feet.

The concrete wall declined in height about every eight to ten feet from the center point and ran about forty more feet along the bank in the other direction of the creek. It was designed to hold up the embankment as it turned the corner and fed into a channel that ran under the street.

Nick took the ceramic idol-thing out of his pocket and

140

held it in his hands, looking at it one final time. A moment later, he took a tight hold of it in his right hand, drew back like a baseball pitcher and flung the ceramic object at the creek wall with all his might.

He nearly fell over into the creek when he thrust the object into the air with all his force into the wall. The object flew through the air and hit the concrete wall about midway up. Upon impact, it exploded into a million pieces.

Nick heard the distinct pop sound of a ceramic object being smashed as it exploded against the wall into a puff of white dust and shrapnel that scattered down into the muddy creek water below. The soppy mud and nasty runoff water sprinkled and splattered, looking like rain drops were hitting it. The remains of the shattered object sprinkled across the dirty water of the creek as the mud below absorbed the tiny shattered ceramic pieces, never to be recovered again.

Nick was satisfied with himself. It was now definitely gone forever. There was no way it was even showing up again, he'd made sure of that. It no longer existed. Not even with super glue and iron determination would anyone ever be able to gather all the pieces and put it back together.

The freaking creepy ass piece of cursed ceramic pottery was no more but forgotten dust. The only evidence that remained of it was the white puff of shattered ceramic dust that stuck to the part of the creek wall where it had impacted. It was nothing but a white smudge on the creek wall that displayed proof that it was destroyed and no longer existed.

It gave Nick a tremendous sense of relief and satisfaction as he walked back up the creek's slope and headed home.

'Enough of that creepy thing.' he thought.

Chapter 9

Nick got home and changed out of his work clothes. He decided to relax for a little while by laying down on top of his bed. Nobody was home. His stepmother and stepsister were probably out visiting family. At least he assumed so, they weren't there and that's where they usually went in the morning if they even got up in the morning at all. Otherwise they usually slept in. But he'd seen that his stepmother's car was gone when he got home.

They must have left when his dad left this morning. That is, just before he showed up at the work site and ruined Nick's day. He'd probably been on a rampage since he got up and they left to escape him for the day.

Nick didn't know how long they'd be gone, but it was fairly safe to assume that it would be for a while. So for the time being he figured it would be safe to relax a bit and lay down. He would take this moment of drama free peace and quiet to figure out what he was going to do today and what his next move would be in terms of finding a new job. There were plenty of local options, he wasn't really concerned too much about it to be honest.

Although he was a little perturbed about the method and manner in which he'd been fired. Notwithstanding the treatment and lack of support from his cowardly co-workers, he was excited he didn't have to get on those stupid hot roofs anymore.

That meant less physical labor and less abuse. The exciting part of it all was that he'd have a chance to get a job where he'd be treated at least like a human being and if not, at least he wouldn't be the focal point of somebody else's stress and shortcomings.

Indeed, Nick was glad to get off those roofs. There had also been a couple of times that he'd almost fell off the roof stepping back too far while working. All in all, things were going to get better. He could feel it.

Nick changed his clothes and then laid on his bed deep in thought. After a moment he heard a soft tapping on the floor past the doorway that led into the vanity and bathroom area. The lights were out and the door to the vanity room was open.

The soft tapping got Nick's attention because the door in the vanity room around the corner that led into the bathroom was closed. The door on the other side of the bathroom which led to his stepsister's room was always closed as well. Nobody ever walked around and used that vanity room other than Nick and his dad, whom only passed through it to use the shower.

Nick lifted his head up from his pillow and looked past his feet towards the vanity where he heard the sound coming from. It was too dark past the doorway leading into the vanity room to see past the darkened pathway that led to the bathroom. Even though it was early in the day, there weren't any windows back there to let any light in.

As he looked on past his feet trying to figure where the noise was coming from, he heard the door handle to the bathroom door start to jiggle. The bathroom door handle was a bit loose and always jiggled when it was turned.

He heard the bathroom door knob jiggle as it turned open in the other room. Nick sat up in the bed, supporting himself with his elbows so he could see who it was.

He heard the bathroom door swing open. It puzzled him because he didn't hear anyone come home. He was pretty sure nobody else was home. He heard the bathroom door swing open and lightly tap against the wall as opened all the way.

No, he wasn't hearing things, that was definitely the bathroom door being opened. Nick looked on into the vanity room and tried to see past the corner as he strained to listen. He half expected his step-sister to come around the corner.

Nobody came around the corner as he expected. He continued looking past the doorway and as he heard soft tapping on the tiled bathroom floor. It was a light tapping sound that sounded almost like tiny footsteps walking heel-toe and it sounded like it was coming closer out of the bathroom.

Nick sat up all the way and reached over to turn on the small lamp that was next to his bed. He switched on light and turned to look into the vanity room.

The lamp barely lit vanity room and he really couldn't see very well in there from his bed. Still, it would have been enough light to see who was there and he seen nobody. But as he looked down towards the floor he seen standing on the tile floor just before the corner was one of Monika's ceramic dolls!

Nick was instantly alarmed.

He leaned forward to get a better look. It was definitely one of his stepsister's creepy ceramic dolls that she had lined up along her bedroom wall.

It was just standing there by itself as if it were alive and able to move around by itself.

He couldn't believe what he was seeing. Did he fall asleep when he was laying on his bed and just dreaming this?

No, he was awake and that thing was definitely standing there unsupported on the vanity floor.

Impossible!

Suddenly, while Nick was staring at it trying to determine if he was really seeing it or not, its head moved and it looked directly up at him.

It blinked its eyes a couple times then said, "my real daddy is dead."

Nick heart sunk as he suddenly went into panic. He was horrified.

148

The doll giggled then turned around by itself ran off towards the bathroom, into the darkness.

Nick could hear its ceramic feet clicking on the tiled floor as it ran through the bathroom and into utility room then into Monika's room.

A second later he heard the door leading to his stepsister's room slam shut.

Nick sat in his bed trembling.

Did that just happen? No way did that just happen.

His heart raced as he felt himself filling with panic as thoughts raced through his mind.

There is no way I can stay in this place any longer, I have to get out of here. What kind of insane crap is this?! There's no way that doll just stood there by itself and talked. And then ran off back into Monika's room! I must be hallucinating or something. None of that just happened. It had to be a delusion. I mean, that was impossible. It did not happen. Someone has to be playing a trick on me. They had to be!

To make it even worse, it was his stepsister Monika's doll and her dad was in fact dead. When Nick first met them, he was told that Monika's dad served in the Army and committed suicide shortly after returning home from war. Monika was just an infant at the time, so she had no memory of him or any of it ever happening.

One day, Nick's stepmother had told him what had really happened. She told him that Monika's dad had put the barrel of a shotgun into his mouth and pulled the trigger. She said his autopsy report said he had a mixture of pain killers, street drugs, and alcohol in his blood at the time of death.

She said that he returned from the Army a changed person and was never the same again. When he came home, he started drinking heavily, doing drugs, and doing dangerous things for adrenaline boosted excitement. One day when he was home alone, he took his own life. When she got home from visiting her mother's with the baby, that was when she discovered his body.

Monika's only memory of what her dad looked like exists from a picture of him that she keeps by her bed. It's a picture of him in his uniform. Monika doesn't know what really happened to her father and was told that he died in the war. Nick had promised never to tell her otherwise so she always kept a positive memory of him.

This was all just too creepy. Dolls just didn't come to life. No way did that just happen.

Nick finally determined that it didn't just happen. Somebody was playing a prank on me. He had to admit, that was a good one. How they got the doll to walk, blink its eyes and talk, he'll probably never know. He didn't see any strings or anything. It appeared to be animate on its own accord, as if it were actually alive. That was definitely a good trick.

They got me. Good prank.

He figured that it probably was Monika. She's probably in her room right now giggling her heart's content. Nick

150

was too quick to think nobody was home just because her mom's car was gone. She was probably home and decided to play a pranks on him.

Nick decided to catch her. He got up from the bed, walked into the vanity room and turned the light on. He looked around for any evidence of strings or something and found nothing. He opened the door to the bathroom and turned on the light. Nothing in there either. He continued past the other bathroom door and went into the laundry room and looked in the closet.

The closet was pretty much unused, holding spare sheets and towels, laundry soaps, an ironing board and such items. He turned and tried the door leading into Monika's room. It was locked as usual. He looked under the door and seen that there weren't any lights on.

However that didn't mean anything, she could be in there with the lights out trying to hide. He put his ear to the door and listened to see if he could hear her in there. Nick figured that she'd most likely be in there giggling about her prank, but he heard nothing.

Still not satisfied, he walked around through the bathroom and back into his room while turning off all the lights behind him. He was going to try her door from the hallway near the stairs. It was never locked unless she was in there.

Nick reached her door and was very quiet, not wanting her to hear him coming so he could quick open the door and surprise her, catching her red-handed.

Nick quietly reached down to check her door to make sure it wasn't locked. He also listened to make sure she didn't go through the other door leading to the bathroom to hide. The door was unlocked, so he quietly turned it and then when the knob was turned all the way, he quickly opened it and looked into her room.

The curtains were open and lit her room up. Nobody was in there. Her bed was made and empty. Maybe she ran out before he got there. Nick looked to see if the door leading to the bathroom was opened, but it was still closed.

He could see along the walls that her creepy ceramic dolls were all still carefully lined up. Including the one he'd seen walking in the vanity room. It sat there with the other dolls, apparently unmoved and untouched. It gave him the creeps and made him real hesitant to even walk any further into the room. His first instinct upon seeing the doll was to leave the room, shut the door and never go near the damn thing.

Yet, he shook off that feeling, still rationalizing that it was just a prank and the doll wasn't really alive. How on Earth could it possibly be. It was just a doll. An inanimate object.

This logical rationalization gave him the confidence to walk further into the room and walk past the dolls to check and make sure the door leading to the bathroom was still locked. If Monika went through it to hide in order to keep her prank going, it would be unlocked. Otherwise she'd have to go through his room to get back.

He walked past the dolls lined up along the wall and

kept his eye on the door, trying to not look at the dolls. They really gave him the creeps and in the back of his mind, he half expected the doll to move or say something. He really didn't like being in there and he hated those creepy dolls.

Nick reached the door and tried the door knob, it was still locked. He turned around, still avoiding looking at the dolls and knelt to look underneath Monika's bed to see if she was hiding there. Nope, nothing there but a line of shoes and flip flops.

Ah-ha! The closet, he thought. She's hiding in the closet. Nick walked over to the closet and opened the door to look in. Nothing in there but her clothes.

He suddenly felt very nervous. Monika wasn't here. Nobody was there but him. Nick had an overwhelming urge to get out of that room as fast as he could and away from those creepy dolls. He turned and looked behind him, half expecting the doll or one of the others to be standing right behind him.

To his relief, they weren't. Nothing was behind him. He turned to head out the door and noticed that the doll he'd seen walking and talking in the vanity room had fallen over face down.

Just a moment ago when he passed by them, it was sat up straight with its back leaning against the wall with the other dolls. Now it was bent down forward on its face.

Yes, it was definitely time to get out of that room. Nick walked up to where it had fallen over and kicked the doll in the head. He heard it giggle as he did. He turned around and quickly walked out of the room, shutting the door behind him. He briefly stood in the hallway and listened for a moment. Everything was quiet, he heard no movement or anything.

Nick quickly went into his room to fetch his hat and wallet and quickly left. He went straight downstairs and out the door. Only pausing long enough to look into the living room one last time to make sure nobody else was home. Nobody was home, he was in the apartment alone and he had the sinking feeling that it was definitely time to get out of there.

Nick went out the door and locked it behind him.

He started to head to Steve's apartment before remembering that he'd left for work and Laura was probably gone for the day as well.

Pausing and looking back at his apartment, Nick decided to go ahead and see if Laura was home anyways. He didn't want to go back in his apartment.

Chapter 10

To Nick's relief, Laura was home. He spent much of the day hanging out with her. As attractive as she was, it wasn't the only thing he liked about her. He really liked spending time with her, just hanging out and doing whatever. They just seemed to just 'click' around each other.

However, she was Steve's girlfriend and he absolutely would not cross those boundaries. But Nick was satisfied with just being her friend. He just wanted to be with her and she seemed to really like being with him. She even mentioned that she couldn't talk with Steve the way she could with him. She's told him that he made her feel comfortable and even mentioned that she wished that she'd met him before she'd met Steve.

Nick couldn't respond to that, it seemed like a tempting invitation to cross forbidden boundaries. He needed to keep a degree of distance as much as he could. He and Laura seemed to be falling for each other and he knew that he shouldn't be spending so much time with her. It would simply be taking away another man's woman and Nick felt wrong about doing that.

But he just couldn't leave. He wanted nothing else but to be with her.

They listened to music and talked much of the day away until Steve came home. Of course, when Steve got home, the party was on. He brought home beer and they played beer games while listening to music much of the rest of the evening.

It was starting to get late and Nick knew that he'd better get home before it was too late. Steve offered for him to just spend the night at his place, but Nick declined. Nick figured it was best to head home, after all he'd hung out there all day anyways. There was no sense in overstaying his welcome anymore than he already had.

With a good beer buzz, but not a real stagger, Nick left their place and headed home. He turned the corner to his apartment and passed the six foot front patio wooden privacy fence that was lined with hedges next to the building. The wind blew past and rattled the leaves on the trees and hedges around him.

Just as he walked past the hedges by the corner of the fence, the wind stopped and he heard somebody whisper, "Nicky" from behind the hedge bush beside him.

A chill ran over him.

Nobody's called him 'Nicky' since his mother died. She was the only one that ever called him that.

He heard it again, someone whispering his name,

'Nicky'.

Startled, Nick nearly jumped out of his skin as he stepped back away from the bush. It sounded just like his mother's voice whispering. She had been dead for almost six years now.

Again, a whisper came from behind the hedge bush saying, "Nicky."

Nick grew angry at this being some kind of cruel joke being played on him by someone hiding behind the bushes or fence. This obviously had to be somebody's sick joke.

Angrily, Nick shoved the branches of the hedges aside expecting to catch the prankster and to let them have it for playing such a cruel joke.

He pulled the bush's neatly trimmed branches to the side and exposed the area behind the bush and fence behind it. There was nobody there.

The porch light around the corner was shining in his eyes and prevented him from seeing behind the hedges completely. Nevertheless, he could still tell there wasn't a person hiding behind the bushes or next to the fence. The porch light that shining around the corner of the fence made it hard to see the front of the fence and shadowed it in darkness. Even still, Nick could see that there was something shiny on the ground at the bottom of the fence behind the bush reflecting the light.

He couldn't see what it was without a flashlight and was way too curious to wait until the morning when the sunlight would illuminate and reveal it. He squatted down by the bush and reached down into the darkness to retrieve it. Fumbling slightly in the darkness, he picked up the glossy object and looked at it in the light.

When he picked it up, it felt familiar to him. It didn't feel very heavy and was cool to the touch, like something made of glass or metal. He pulled his hand back out of the bushes and stood back up. When he turned into the light to see what it was, he froze petrified in horror. It was that demon looking ceramic object that he smashed into the creek's concrete wall.

"Whoa! No way! I smashed it to pieces. It was smashed!"

He knew it was smashed, he'd seen the pieces shatter everywhere and go flying in the air in every direction. He even watched them fall into the deep loose mud that filled that part of the creek bed. This thing did not even exist anymore, yet here it was in his hand.

Nick couldn't believe it. If he wasn't holding it in his own hands, he definitely would have never believed it.

A cold shudder ran down his back and through his whole body. He felt this thing was alive somehow and following him. He felt it was messing with his head as well. It gave him chills to actually be holding this thing. It truly was some kind of supernatural object. That can be the only explanation. This thing was somehow alive, it was inherently evil, and it was definitely following him.

It ultimately refused to be destroyed nor would go away. He knew this was the message that it was trying to give him: that he could not rid himself of it. It wouldn't

160

allow him to be rid of it and it wanted him to clearly know that.

Nick felt overwhelmed with panic. He didn't know what to do.

Frightful and filled with anger, he tightly grasped the object in his hand and turned around quickly, half expecting something to be standing behind him to confront him face to face.

Nothing was there but the reaching darkness past where the hedges blocked the porch light from being lit and allowing him to see past.

Nick stormed forward with an angry determination. Feeling threatened and helpless against this unseen, unknown thing that would not leave him be. He marched onto the darkened sidewalk leading to where the parking lot was. He reached the asphalt parking lot and continued walking across the street and onto the grass that was on the other side, which led to where the creek was located.

He could only see blackness in front of him, but he knew the creek and tall grass were there. With all his might and in an almost rage, he threw the cold ceramic object into the darkness and immediately turned away to walk back to the apartment.

The wind had suddenly picked up just as he threw the object into the darkness and he did not hear whether or where it had landed. He didn't want to know, he didn't care.

Nick marched back at a steady and determined pace,

ignoring the taunting darkness around him. Why should he be bothered with the darkness, it wouldn't leave him alone. He continued walking towards the poorly lit sidewalk path on the other side of the parking lot. Feeling an overwhelming sense of fear and helplessness, he blocked out these feelings and ignored everything around him in his mind as he marched up the walkway to his front door.

He got to the front door and turned the knob, checking to see if it was locked while he reached into his pocket to fetch his house key with his other hand.

To his surprise, the door was already unlocked. His heart instantly sank and he feared that his dad may already be home and sitting there on the couch, watching TV, facing the front door where he'd have to confront him. Nick really wasn't in the mood for that and hoped that he was wrong.

He opened the door and entered the apartment, ready for and expecting instant drama. Monika, his 13 year old step-sister was sitting in the living room on the couch watching music videos on TV.

Nick knew nobody else was home, because she wasn't allowed to watch the music videos. Both his dad and her mother hated watching or even listening to them.

Nick shut the front door and locked it it behind him. He turned back facing Monika and waved at her. Monika was painting her toe nails with her feet on the coffee table. Another sign their parents weren't home as she wouldn't be painting her toenails in the living room or putting her feet on the coffee table.

Monika looked up at him while still holding the nail polish applicator in her hand and stuck her middle finger up at him. She snapped her gum and then returned to painting her toe nails.

Monika and Nick never hit it off very well. They both had a silent mutual distaste for each other. Nevertheless, Nick was relieved to discover that neither his dad nor stepmother were home yet. He felt relieved and took his jacket off. He flipped on the light over the stairwell and went up the stairs, taking them two at a time and entered his bedroom.

The light going into the shared bathroom was still on. Obviously left on by whoever had last been in there, most likely his step-sister. She had a habit of never turning lights off. Nevertheless, Nick was usually the one blamed for wasting electricity. The light over the bathroom's vanity mirror stretched across the entirety of the two sink vanity. It put out enough light to illuminate Nick's bedroom with its fluorescent brilliance.

Nick flicked on his bedroom overhead light, which gave the remainder of his room an orange glow from the low wattage incandescent light bulb that was mounted in the ceiling fixture. The overhead light bulb suddenly started to dim and then went out completely a few seconds after being turned on as he crossed the room towards his bed. Nick tossed his jacket on the bed and looked up at the ceiling light just as it burnt out completely.

He walked back to the wall switch and flicked it off and on again. He clicked the wall switch on and off a few times before giving up as he cursed under his breath and walked a few steps towards his bed to kick his shoes off onto the floor near the corner of the bed.

Needing a shower, he walked through the vanity room, which led into the shared bathroom and went in to take a shower.

Nick stood in the shower and allowed the hot water to run over his head and flow over his entire body. The water that flowed over was warm and comforting, the heat relaxed his shoulders and sore back. He was oblivious to anything that was going on in the world outside of the shower.

He'd just washed his hair and was nearly done in the shower when he heard one of the bathroom doors open.

The bathroom had two doors leading from each side of the apartment from both upstairs bedrooms that were adjoined to it.

Thinking it was probably his stepsister, Nick called out, "I'm in here."

After he called out he seen a large shadow on the other side of the shower curtain. Someone was in the bathroom with him and it wasn't his stepsister. The shadow he seen through the shower curtain was that of a full sized man.

Nick nervously called out again, "hello?"

The shower curtain suddenly pulled open.

Startled, Nick quickly turned his head to see who it was.

It was his dad.

"Get the fuck out of the shower!" His dad yelled as he reached in and grabbed a handful of Nick's wet hair and pulled him out of the shower by it.

Vulnerable and shocked by being suddenly yanked out of the shower by his hair, Nick tripped over the bathtub's slippery side and fell to his side.

His dad continued to pull him out of the shower by his hair. Nick's feet slid helplessly across the floor as he desperately tried to gain his footing and stand up.

Nick was naked and drenched from the shower. The floor was becoming soaking wet from the water dripping off his body and from the shower head which was still fully spraying water through its jets.

His dad pulled him up to an almost standing position and with his free hand punched Nick on the side of the head above his left ear. The force of the blow knocked him flying backwards as his bare feet slipped on the wet bathroom floor tile.

No longer being held up by his hair, Nick flipped backwards onto the bathroom floor and hit his head on the side of the bathtub which knocked him unconscious.

He was only momentary blacked out. He woke laying on his back on the bathroom floor with his head cocked up and leaning against the side of the bathtub. The warm water from the shower hitting him and soaking the bathroom floor around him.

Nick started to get up and suddenly felt his head begin to pound. It felt like the pressure was going to make his eyeballs pop out. He nearly vomited from the feeling.

He sat up and propped himself up in a sitting position for a moment while the feeling of nausea passed. His head was still throbbing in pain from hitting the bathtub. He struggled up to his knees and reached over to turn the shower water off.

After a moment, Nick's head starting to clear up. He looked around in the bathroom. The bathroom doors were both shut and locked. His dad was not in there or anywhere around. The bathroom floor was soaking wet. He scrambled to get up and grab a towel that was hanging on the towel rack. He had to sop up the water before anyone seen that the floor was soaked. It was the only shower in the house and everyone used it. Someone would surely see it and he'd indubitably get in trouble over it, no matter as to what or why.

He threw the towel on the floor then got on his hands and knees to soak up the water. Getting most of the water absorbed into the towel, Nick took the drenched towel and tossed it into the bathtub. He grabbed a second towel that was hanging on the rack and toweled himself dry.

When he toweled his hair dry, the side of his head hurt just above his ear and the back of his head. He pulled the towel from over his head and noticed it had blood on it. His head was obviously bleeding somewhere. Nick looked down on the floor and didn't see any blood on the white tiled floor. He wrapped the towel around his waist and

166

knelt beside the bathtub and grabbed the soaked towel he used to sop the water off from the floor. He wrung the water from out of the towel then quickly re-wrapped it and wrung it out again several more times.

Nick tried to get as much water out of the towel as hastily as he could. He tossed the wrung out towel back on the floor and mopped up the last remaining puddles of water from the bathroom floor and then opened the opposite bathroom door which led to the laundry room. He grabbed the wet towel from the floor and tossed it in the open the washing machine.

Nick still wasn't sure what had just happened and wouldn't have believed that it happened if he hadn't seen the blood and felt the injuries.

Maybe it didn't happen and he just blacked out, fell on the floor and dreaming this all as happening while he was briefly unconscious. But his skull also ached where his hair had been pulled. If it didn't really happen, then how did he get a banged up head and his hair pulled?

He walked back into the bathroom and shut the door behind him and opened the door on the opposite side of the bathroom which led into the vanity room towards his bedroom.

He turned the lights off and shut the doors behind him as he entered his darkened room and flipped on the switch to the ceiling light. The light didn't turn on and he instantly remembered that it had blown out just before he went to take a shower.

Cussing under his breath, Nick walked across the bedroom towards the opposite end where the bedroom closet was located. He kept his hands out in front of him as he walked. carefully trying not to trip over his shoes or walk into the bed. Slowly he crossed the darkened room, regretting having turned off all the lights behind him and shutting the door.

Still damp from his shower, Nick was starting to get a chill and was getting goosebumps on his skin. He couldn't help the feeling that something was in the room with him. It felt as if someone were watching him in the dark.

Nick reached the other side of the room and felt the hinge part of the closet door with one hand and the wall with his other hand in front of him. He knew the layout of the room, so he moved his hand across the surface of the closet door until he touched the trim of the door frame.

He moved his hand up and down the wall next to the door until he located the closet light switch on the wall and flicked it on. The closet light turned on and the light illuminated from under and around the closet door. He reached down with his other hand and felt for the doorknob to open the closet door.

As the closet door swung open, Nick was hit by a burst of cold air that rushed out of the closet with a flash of bright white light. The whoosh of cold air blasting past him had stunned him while the flash of light blinded him at the same time.

Then as fast as it happened, it was gone.

Nick stood in bathed in the light of the open doorway of the closet. It took him a moment to open his eyes and look around. He was still partially blinded by the flash of light and was now shivering from the burst of cold. He stood there for a moment waiting for his eyes to adjust.

The momentary light blindness quickly faded and Nick was able to see around the room. It was then that he heard the front door slam shut downstairs. He also felt it shut through the floor.

He stood there quietly listening and then he heard his father's slurred voice muffled through the floor as he yelled at his stepsister downstairs.

"What the hell are you doing in the living room with that shit?! And get that shit off my TV!"

Wait a second, Nick thought. If his dad was just now coming home, then who hit him in the bathroom?

Nick felt the back of his head with his hand and cringed from the pain as soon as he touched it. Yeah, it really happened. He really hit the floor and his hair had really been pulled. The side of his head was throbbing from where he'd been hit, he didn't just dream it up.

Nick heard the familiar footsteps of his stepsister running up the stairs and then the sound of her bedroom door shutting.

No surprise there, he thought.

A moment later, he heard his dad's voice suddenly get louder, as if he were at the base of the stairs. A second later

Nick heard the sound of his father's footsteps as he made his way up the stairs.

Nick's heart suddenly started to race in panic as he grabbed the towel that he had wrapped around his waist and tossed it on the closet floor. He quickly turned around and rushed across the room, leaving the closet light on and door still open behind him. He leapt into his bed while scrambling on his hands and knees to get under the covers and pretend he was asleep. He figured if his dad thought he was asleep then maybe he'd leave him alone. At least that was the hasty plan.

Just as Nick was about to get under the bed covers, his bedroom door flew open and the ceiling light turned on.

It was his dad and as soon as he seen that Nick was bare naked and on his hands and knees with his backside towards him, he immediately flew into a rage.

"What the fuck are you doing!?" his dad angrily shouted.

Without answering, Nick grabbed the top of his bed cover and quickly threw his body under it and pulled the blanket over him. He tried to quickly concealed his nakedness under the blanket as he pulled them up to his chest.

Still in his fit of rage, Nick's dad turned around and stormed out of the room, leaving the door still open and light on. Nick heard him quickly stomping down the stairs, cussing the whole way and then open the door downstairs into his room. Still hearing him yelling and cussing, Nick heard him emerge out of his room downstairs and storm back up the stairs.

His heart pounded as he heard the approaching steps of his father coming up the stairs, cussing at him at the top of his lungs for all in the house and probably the neighbors to hear.

His dad emerged in the bedroom doorway holding a double barrel shotgun.

Nick immediately cried out in panic, "No! Don't shoot me!"

His dad held the shotgun in both hands with the barrels cocked open and then slammed the shotgun barrels closed.

"Please!" Nick started to openly weep, tears rolling down his face. "Please, please don't hurt me!"

His dad approached the side of his bed.

"You naked! Pathetic! Crying sissy!" He reached down and grabbed Nick by his hair, pulling him out of the bed.

Nick reached up and held his dad's hand that was grasping his hair in an attempt to stand up so he wouldn't be dragged around by his hair.

Upon feeling Nick's hands touch his hand, his dad threw him on the floor.

"Do not touch me with your filthy faggot hands ever again!"

His dad held the shotgun up in front of Nick's face.

"Do you want me to bash in your fucking face in with this?!" he screamed at him, spraying some spittle in Nick's face.

Nick continued to sob in fear, holding his hands up defensively as his father started to kick him in the legs and stomach. While still holding the shotgun in his other hand, he then punched Nick squarely in the face and knocked him backwards onto the floor.

When he swung at Nick, he pulled a muscle in his shoulder. This only made him angrier.

Nick felt the powerful slam on his face by his father's fist one last time and the world around him begin to blacken. Everything was in a haze of blackness with an explosion of white specks everywhere as he hit the floor behind him. Nick felt his face numb up as he laid on his back still seeing stars and hearing his dad cussing in pain about his arm.

Nick looked up and could see his dad thrashing about in the room, holding his arm in pain until he stomped out, slamming the bedroom door shut behind him.

He laid his head back and looked up at the ceiling, stunned. He could hear his dad still cussing as he stomped down the stairs and then slam the door to his bedroom. He could still hear the muffled sounds of his father cussing.

Nick laid there in shock and stared at the ceiling, blinking his eyes in disbelief. All he heard now was ringing in his ears as the room began to fade away and darken in the corners of his sight. As everything began to fade away

and the ringing in his ears got louder, Nick felt someone
breathing their hot breath into his face. Each breath he felt
on him felt like pure hatred. He could not see if anyone
was in his face, but with each pulse of breath that hit him,
he felt himself fade away.

The darkness slowly encircled him as he drifted into
unconsciousness.

Chapter 11

Nick woke up to the sound of obnoxious blasting coming from his alarm clock. He didn't remember setting the alarm on the clock, but he quickly scurried across the floor to turn it off before it woke anyone else up.

He sat up and leaned against his bed. He looked at where he woke up and found that he'd been laying naked in the middle of his bedroom floor all night. He instantly remembered what had happened last night.

Still groggy, he looked about the room as he tried to wake up fully. The ceiling light that failed when he tried to turn it on last night, but turned on when his dad came in, was still on and so was the closet light.

Nick stood up and walked to his dresser to grab a pair of underwear out of one the drawers. He also pulled out a pair of socks. Closing the dresser drawer, he weakly sat down on the floor and began getting dressed. He got up and grabbed a pair of jeans that were tossed on the closet floor.

After he finished dressing, he went into the bathroom

and seen his battered face in the mirror. He walked up to the vanity and examined his face in the mirror more closely. His nose was slightly swollen and red, but it didn't look like it was broken.

Nick's forehead and around his eyes were red and slightly swollen. Both eyes were bloodshot and red. He felt the back of his head and remembered the incident in the bathroom and suddenly began to feel afraid.

He had to get out of here.

He reached over and grabbed a hair brush and quickly brushed his hair, being mindful of the sore spots on his head. He wet his hair in a place or two to get it to lay down properly, then turned around and went back in his room. Nick sat down on the floor and put his shoes on, nervously looking around in the room.

He got up, grabbed his wallet and house key, stuffing them into his pockets as he grabbed his jacket and headed out of his room. He turning off the light and shut the door behind him and then stood there quietly for a moment. He listened intently to make sure nobody else was awake or downstairs before he went down there.

Once he felt confident that nobody else was up and about, Nick quietly went down the stairs. When he reached bottom of the stairs, he paused a moment to listen again to make sure that nobody else was up yet.

He unlocked the front door and quietly went out, closing and locking it back behind him.

Nick stood there for a moment, relived to have got out,

trying to decide what to do. It was early in the morning on a Saturday.

He decided to walk over to Steve and Laura's apartment and see if they were up yet, but there wasn't an answer at the door.

Nick stood there in front of their door for a moment thinking about where he should go. He definitely didn't want to go back home and nobody was up yet.

He noticed the shade in the neighbor's window briefly peek open. They probably thought he was going to try to break in the apartment or something. Not wanting to make them any more nervous than they probably already were, Nick began walking.

He didn't know where he was going, but he was definitely headed in that direction.

Nick walked through the apartment complex until he got to the main road where the business strip was. It was still early and none of the businesses were open yet. He crossed the street and continued walking. He figured he could probably go hang out at the library for a bit and if not, perhaps something else along the way may catch his attention. At the moment, he really didn't care.

He walked until the library was just a few more blocks down the street. The street he'd been walking on had a cemetery along the other side of the road. He could take a shortcut through the cemetery, but he never felt comfortable walking through graveyards.

Not that he was afraid of spooks or anything like that,

he just felt it was disrespectful to do so. Besides, he wanted to stop by the doughnut shop that was on the corner at the end of the street. He always had a bit of a sweet tooth and loved the nut covered chocolate bars they had.

As Nick continued walking down the street, he noticed an old lady walking in the opposite direction towards him. He tried not to really look at her and kept his head slightly down. He didn't want to intimidate her or make her think he was a threat of any kind.

As he got closer to her, he noticed that she was a bit overdressed by wearing a heavy coat and hat. She seemed like she was bundled up for winter. It was a little chilly this morning, but really nothing that would require more than a light jacket. Nick just smiled to himself knowing how some old people get cold easily.

When he got closer to her and was about to pass her, Nick smiled and nodded politely as he continued to walk. She looked back up at him with her aged eyes and smiled. Nick was sure she could barely see him. Being friendly Nick smiled back at her and said, "hello."

She smiled back warmly as elderly people tended to do and greeted him back saying, "hello, young man."

Nick smiled and then looked away, as he passed her and continued to walk down the street.

After he passed her, he suddenly felt a tug on his sleeve from behind. It was a direct tug that pulled him back slightly, stopping him in his tracks. It was the old lady.

'What the hell was wrong with this old lady?' he thought.

She tugged hard on his sleeve, pulling him down to her level. Before he was able to turn head to look, he heard her loudly whisper into his ear, "I know what you are and I will burn you!"

She let go of his sleeve and Nick turned to look at her. She looked angry and her eyes were scolding with hatred and fury.

'Who the hell was this crazy old lady? Just a second ago, she was this sweet grandmother type with a warm friendly smile. And now she was an angry, crazed woman from who knows where or what and what in the world she was talking about.'

Figuring that she was just old and probably demented, Nick turned and walked away from her. After he took a few hurried steps, he looked back over his shoulder to make sure she wasn't following him and she was gone.

Just like that,..gone.

Nick stopped walking and turned completely around, looking around for her. She was nowhere to be found. She was a feeble old lady and this made no sense at all. When he was walking down the street and approaching her, she had a real slow and labored pace. There was no way she could have just suddenly ran down the street or even to a nearby house that fast. He only took a couple of steps before looking back and she simply wasn't there anymore. It was as if she never was there in the first place.

Still looking around bewildered, Nick stood there a moment trying to figure out what just happened.

Nick turned back around and started walking down the

street again. A bit startled and not sure what to make of all, he picked up his pace as his mind raced.

"Did I just see a ghost or something? In broad daylight? Naw, that's silly superstitious crap anyways. I mean really.. of all ghosts that could be out there, I get the crazy old lady one that says she 'knows what I am and that she'll burn me.' What was that suppose to mean anyways? It's not like it was the 15th century and I was someone accused of witchcraft after all. What did she think I was anyways?"

To Nick's relief, he arrived at the doughnut shop. He went inside and was fortunate enough that there was one more chocolate covered nut bar left.

Although they had seats and small tables in the doughnut shop, Nick decided to eat outdoors. He tossed his napkin in the trash can and decided to just walk back to the apartment complex. Perhaps he'd find someone he knew was up and around. Maybe Steve or Laura were up or back from wherever they went.

Nick walked back the way he'd came, keeping a watchful eye out for crazy old ladies. He figured, if one showed up this time he was just going to cross the street and walk next to the cemetery and avoid them straight out.

It wasn't very long until he reached the apartment complex. Just in case that crazy old lady did show back up, he walked at a much quicker pace then before.

Nick weaved his way through the apartment complex until he was walking around the corner to Steve and Laura's apartment again. He could hear music blasting in the direction of their apartment. Yep, Steve was definitely home now.

Nick figured he'd knock on his door and hang out with him for a bit. But before so, he remembered that Steve wanted to borrow some of his music. His dad would be gone by now, so he could go up and fetch them from his room and then bring them over with him.

Nick walked around the corner leading to his apartment and peek around the corner to see if his dad's truck was there or not.

It was there, parked in its usual spot. His dad was home.

'Damn. So much for that idea,' he thought. *'I'm not going in there after that crazy shit last night and with the doll the day before. Something very wrong is going on in that place.'*

He definitely feel safe being there any longer, no matter what was going on. Not to mention crazy old ladies walking down the street that disappeared in thin air. Nick felt like he had to be losing his mind.

He was just about to turn around and walk back the way he came when he noticed his stepsister sitting next to the building. She was sitting on the ground with her knees up and her head buried in her arms.

She was crying.

Nick walked up to her to see if she was okay and to find out why she was sitting there crying in the first place.

"Monika? Are you okay?"

She lifted her head up and looked at him. Her eyes were puffy from crying and on her forehead, Nick could see a huge reddened knot.

"What happened to your head?”

She leaned forward and threw her arms around him, burying her face in his shoulders almost knocking him backwards.

Nick put his arms around her and asked again, “What happened to you.”

She just continued sobbing for a moment, not answering. Nick was starting to get worried. He pulled her slightly back and looked her in the eyes.

“Monika, please tell me what happened? It's okay, you can tell me,” he reassured her.

She stopped sobbing for a moment and spoke in a shaky voice, “your dad.”

She stopped short of what she was going to say and started crying again.

“My dad, what?”

She stopped crying and said, “I was on the phone and your dad came home. He was already drunk and started yelling at me about being on the phone.”

"What did he say?"

“He said, 'what the fuck are you doing? Calling up those boys?!'”

Nick nodded. He knew how his dad was.

"I said that I wasn't." she continued. "I told him I was on the phone with a girl friend from school."

She started sobbing again as she tried to speak then said, "he walked over to me and slapped the phone out of my hand. When he did that, he hit me in the face with his hand and the phone at the same time."

Nick shook his head in disbelief. "Wow."

"After that, I ran upstairs to my room."

"Is that how you got a bump on your head?"

She shook her head and sobbed, "no."

"After I ran in my room, I heard him coming up the stairs yelling at me about boys and being a whore. He kicked my bedroom door open. It wasn't even locked," she pointed out and started crying again.

She then said, "he was standing there yelling at me and was holding his shotgun."

Nick was shocked to hear this.

'No way did he do to her what he did to me.'

Nick's heart started to thump as anger began boiling inside of him. He looked at her and asked, "he did what?"

She stressed, "his shotgun, the one that has the two barrels on it."

Nick nodded, "Yes, I now the one."

"He waved it around and threatened me with it."

Nick could feel himself getting even angrier. He tried not to let Monika see this.

"Then he took the barrel off of it and hit me on the head with it."

She turned her head up slightly and touched the knot on her forehead, showing him where.

"He hit me right here with it," she said as she indicated the spot and then started crying again.

Nick's heart was pounding hard at this time, not from fear but out of pure anger.

'How the hell could he do that to her. It was one thing to hit and take out his anger on me, but it was another thing for him to hit her. This can't be tolerated. This will not be tolerated, I have to do something. He's not going to get away with this.'

Nick looked back down at her. She was crying hysterically and starting to tremble. He had to make sure she was okay.

"Come with me. We have to make sure you're okay." He explained as they walked towards Steve and Laura's apartment around the corner.

Nick knocked on their door and Steve answered. As soon as he seen us, he knew something was wrong and asked, "what's the matter? What happened?"

Steve stepped aside and motioned for them to come in.

"My dad hit her. Can I use your phone?"

"Yeah dude, of course. It's right there by the couch."

184

Nick used his telephone and dialed the emergency number 9-1-1. He told them his stepsister was hurt and that she'd been hit with a shotgun barrel.

It wasn't long until both the police and an ambulance showed up.

The paramedics gathered Monika and treated her wound inside their ambulance. The police questioned Nick about what had happened. Nick told them everything that had happened since he found her sitting by the building. He didn't think to tell them about what happened to him personally the night before.

The police instructed Nick to wait at Steve's apartment as they went to question Monika.

As they walked to the ambulance, Nick seen his dad walk out to his truck and then start to walking back to the apartment. Nick backed up and went into Steve's apartment so he wouldn't see him.

The police intercepted him as he was walking back towards the apartment and were now questioning his dad.

After a few minutes, Monika was bandaged and released by the paramedics with a cold pack on her head. An officer escorted her back to their apartment and Nick assumed they were questioning her there. He remained hidden at Steve's apartment. He didn't think it would be safe for him to go there right now. Police or not, especially when he was the one who called them.

Nick stayed inside Steve's apartment and anxiously waited to see what happened. He assumed his dad would be arrested. This all was happening so fast.

'What just happened here?' Nick's mind anxiously raced as he became more and more nervous. Steve tried to calm him down and relax to no avail.

After a while, a police officer came to Steve's door and asked to talk to Nick. Steve let him in.

"I'm Officer Richards. Okay, let me just give you guys a quick run down at what we've got. Your sister says that she got the bump on her head from running up the stairs and falling. She claims that when she fell, she hit the wall and that's what caused the mark on her forehead. The paramedics say she'll be fine, but should still follow up at the emergency room so a doctor can make certain."

The officer looked up them from his clipboard and could tell they were flabbergasted.

"I'm sorry guys. But if she says it was an accident, we have to go by that."

"Hey, what about that guy they found in the dumpster?"

The officer looked at him for a moment and then said, "it looks like a homicide. the guy has defensive wounds on him. He fought for his life."

"Wow, that's crazy. Have they found who did it?"

"I'm not at liberty to say." He paused a moment and noticed the bruises on Nick. "How did you get those marks on you?"

Nick hesitated for a moment and then reluctantly

answered, "my dad."

The officer shook his head. "I bet you fell down some stairs too. Your sister's going to be alright. My advice is to call social services. Our hands are tied unless she tells us what really happened."

The officer apologized one last time and then left.

Nick was beside himself in complete disbelief of what just happened. There was no way he could go back home now. Not after calling the police on his dad. He really didn't think this through or at least he didn't expect her to suddenly lie and change her story to the police.

'I was only trying to help her, what else was I suppose to do> Now I'm in real danger for calling the police on him. What am I going to do now?'

Chapter 12

Unsure where to really go, Nick went to Joe's place, a friend he met in school that lived on the other side of town. It was a run down part of the city that was plagued by crime, poverty, and unemployment. The part of town that people intentionally avoided, especially at night.

His friend's apartment was a small efficiency kind of unit. It was located in an old building with eight small rundown apartment units located above a sealed and abandoned downstairs business area. It was obvious that the business shops hadn't been used in years. The windows were all boarded up where the shops once were.

The apartments were old and largely neglected, the smell of mold and old dust hung in the air. That musty kind of smell that never seemed to go away from carpeting that was older than most of the tenants that resided there. The apartments themselves were partially furnished by old worn out furniture that had been left behind by previous tenants over the years.

Nick's friend, Joe was related to the building's apartment manager, his Uncle Sam, who just happened to be an unemployed drunkard.

Joe was a couple of years older than Nick. Joe had quit school and moved into his uncle's apartment complex. When he moved in, he helped clean the apartment units up to make them available for renting.

Everything in the apartment units were old and very outdated. The old style bathtubs in each unit had their edges worn from decades of use. The vanity style sinks had rust spots left where the leaking spigots had dripped and eroded them way past the enamel paint that originally coated them. All the apartment's fixtures were actually various outdoor looking or utility types of spigots. Each sink and bathtub had two spigots mounted left and right of each other. Which side spigot was the hot or cold water varied and greatly depended on which sink or tub was being used.

Joe's uncle knew practically nothing about plumbing or maintenance in the slightest bit. So sometimes the hot water spigot was on the left side and sometimes it was the one on the right side. Nick was already familiar with all of this because he'd come over a few times before to help Joe do some of the cleaning or maintenance in the apartment units.

Nick arrived at Joe's apartment hoping that he could stay a few nights. He'd stayed over a night or two before in the past. He was also hoping that Joe would talk to his uncle about letting him rent one of the apartments. That is, once he got a job and a paycheck coming in.

Joe asked his uncle and he agreed to give Nick one of

the apartments midway down the hall on the street side.

Nick was thankful that it was already partially furnished from the previous tenants that had been there before. He wasn't looking forward to having to sleep on the floor of an unfurnished apartment with just the clothes on his back.

It was a dirty apartment with a stained coffee table and hide-a-bed couch. There was also a couple of vinyl chairs. One of chairs had the middle cushion split out in the middle and had been repaired by duct tape. There was also a dinette set in the small dining room that was connected the small kitchenette and a small dressing room which led to the bathroom. The kitchenette already had a mixed variety of plates, bowls, and various cookware.

Everything was all dusty and needing to be cleaned of course, but all were usable. The refrigerator was as old as the dinette set. An old but running refrigerator of a style they haven't made in decades. The freezer part inside of it was the type that would often freeze over, requiring frequent manual defrosting. There was a rusty screw driver on top of the refrigerator most likely there for just that very purpose.

Joe's uncle agreed to let Nick use the apartment free for the first month with no deposit, but he had to start paying rent the following month.

This was something Nick felt he could do. He just had to find a job. He really didn't feel that it would be too much of a problem. Surely he'd be able to find a job in a day or two. He didn't have a car, but there were plenty of places within walking distance. All low wage jobs, but really that's all he was going to find at the moment.

Unfortunately that was something he'd have to wait a couple of days on. It was Friday night and it was always better to show up to apply when the managers were in.

He was willing to wash dishes to make the rent money if he had to. The rent for the run down apartment was cheap enough and he had all the world of confidence that he'd be able to do it.

He spent much of the evening relaxing until there was a knock on the door. Nick wasn't expecting anyone, but he figured that it was probably Joe or his uncle and got up to answer the door.

To Nick's surprise, it was Laura at the door.

This was indeed quite a surprise, he absolutely didn't expect to see her here or at this hour. Perhaps Steve had told her what happened and she came to make sure everything was okay. After his sister had changed her story after he called the police, Nick didn't stay around very long and had left before she had came home.

Breaking the awkward moment of Nick standing at the door puzzled, Laura greeted him.

"Hi!"

"Hey." Nick was still a little puzzled.

"I heard you were here. Can I come in?"

"Oh yes! Sorry. Please, come in to my humble

commode,..I mean abode." said Nick as he stepped aside and let her in.

Nick quickly looked up and down the hall to see if anyone was with her, expecting to see Steve walking down the hall.

She was alone. Nick shut the door behind her.

"How's it goi -" As soon he turned around, she walked over and embraced him with a hug before he could finish speaking.

He hugged her back and then after a moment of silent hugging, Nick asked her if she was alright.

She released him and looked down so he couldn't see her eyes, nodding her head.

"I'm fine."

Noticing his mess, Nick quickly scrambled to pick up the blanket he had on the couch.

"Please sit down." he offered, tossing the blanket on one of the chairs.

She sat down on the couch while Nick sat in the chair next to her. Remembering his manners, he asked her if she wanted anything to drink but she declined.

Nick was glad to see Laura, he still secretly held her in his heart and with all the things happening recently, her being there was a welcomed relief.

"Steve broke up with me." she finally announced after a moment.

"Oh? What happened?" Nick pretended to be surprised.

"Yes, I didn't even see it coming, but I probably should have. I just never thought about it. He was finishing with that machinist trade school and, I don't know, I just thought he was going to get a job locally."

"He's not?"

"No, he said he was returning home and that I couldn't come with him." A tear formed in the corner of her eye.

"Wow," Nick exclaimed, not really knowing what to say.

"He said he cleared his apartment's lease and was supposed to have the apartment vacated so the apartment management could clean it in order to rent it to another tenant. He said, so he gets his deposit back."

Still unsure what to say, Nick just shook his head.

"Is it alright of I stay here for a little while?" she suddenly asked Nick, touching him on the arm. He looked up at her openly surprised. He didn't expect her to ask him such a thing. He didn't' even expect to see her here or in all truth, if ever again with everything happening.

"Just for a little while until I can find a job and get on my own feet. " she reassured him.

Nick was overwhelmed with this request, this was a dream come true.

"Of course you can stay." he told her.

'Are you kidding me, I worship the very ground you walk on.' he thought as he smiled to himself.

He'd been deeply in love with her since the first day he seen her, but was never able to express it to her because of her already being in a relationship with his friend Steve.

But now she wasn't with Steve or anyone and here she was. But she was here as a friend and Nick never expressed his feelings to her. But could he do that now? She needed help and he feared that if she didn't feel the same for him then it would just make her very uncomfortable. That was something he didn't want to do to her, something he wouldn't do to her. He couldn't express his feelings to her unless he was sure she felt the same way about him. If she didn't feel the same for him, he was afraid it would destroy their friendship.

"Of course you can stay, you're always welcome with me." Nick said. "Let me show you the apartment."

He gave her the nickel tour of the dinky apartment. It took the whole of two minutes, there wasn't much to show.

"I really appreciate you letting me stay here with you. I promise I'll get a job fast."

"Don't sweat it, you're welcomed to stay as long as you like. My place is yours."

Outside a car horn blasted just outside the window. Someone was honking their car horn in front of the building.

Laura rose up from her seat and said, "Nina's waiting on me outside. I asked her to wait in case I couldn't find you."

"I understand." Nick said.

"She has my stuff in her car. I'll be right back, please wait here."

"Do you need any help?"

"No, but thanks. Please just wait here, I'll be right back."

Laura raced out the door and closed it behind her. After a moment, curiosity took over and Nick rose up out of his chair and walked to look out the window. He seen Nina's car idling in the front parking lot. Laura was down there talking to her while she was grabbing her bags out of the backseat.

Nina looked up at the window and seen Nick looking down at them and waved at him. He smiled and waved back excitedly. A moment later, he seen Laura step away from Nina's car and wave as she drove off, honking her horn a couple of times as she pulled away.

Nick listened at the door for Laura to come back up when he heard a door opening in the apartment building's main corridor. It sounded like it was coming from the direction of the hall where the manager and Joe's apartment doors were located.

Not that he was really concerned, but in a way he hoped it was neither of them. Just as he was thinking this, he heard the Joe's Uncle Sam greeting Laura as she walked down the hallway carrying her bags. Nick quickly opened the door to go help her out and make an attempt to veer her away from him.

Nick didn't know how Sam would react to him having someone stay with him when he hadn't even paid him a single cent in rent yet. Nick didn't want him to think he was taking advantage of him. He thought it best to try to intercept them.

As soon as Nick opened the door, Sam and Laura meet face to face right in front of my his door. He was too late.

"Hi! I'm Sam, the apartment manager. Can I help you?"

"Hello. I'm Laura. Nick's friend." She motion to Nick who was standing in the doorway with a blank look on his face.

She set one of her bags down on the floor and extended her hand to shake Sam's hand.

"What's with all the bags?" Sam inquired.

"Damn," Nick thought. "He's already snooping."

"Well, I just broke up with my boyfriend and I sort of just showed up here on Nick unexpectedly." She smiled and winked at Nick. "He's going to let me stay with him for a few days until I find a job."

Nick, who was now standing beside them, nodded in agreement as he reached down to pick up the bag Laura had set down. He was hoping to put a quick end to the conversation and steer her inside the apartment.

"I still have a couple of apartment units available. I can give you the same deal I gave Nick here." he said, pointing his thumb at Nick.

"Oh, could you? That would be wonderful!" Laura became excited.

Nick just stood there taking it all in. He wasn't sure what to think about this.

'I must have the worse luck in the world.' he thought.

"Hold on and I'll get the key to the apartment on the end over there."

Sam quickly walked down the hall towards his apartment and went inside.

"Isn't this great! I'm so excited." Laura said as she turned towards Nick. "I was really worried about what I was going to do, But now, it looks like things are going to work out."

Nick wanted to try and convince Laura to not get the other apartment and just stay with him, but before he could really say anything, Sam came back with the key and walked them down the hall to the corner apartment.

Sam explained the terms to her as we walked down the hall.

"I'll let you have the apartment deposit free and no rent for the first month, but like him, I expect the rent to be paid next month and on time."

"I really, really appreciate what you're doing for me. I promise I'll have the rent to you on time."

Sam unlocked the apartment door and opened it. He removed the door key and handed it to Laura, who took the key and followed him in the apartment.

"The power should still be on in this apartment," he flicked the wall switch and the ceiling light came on. "Yep." He walked through the apartment and turned on the ceiling light in the kitchenette area.

"There aren't any shades in the kitchen windows, but you can close the blinds in the living room."

"Oh, I am sure I will be fine."

He walked back into the living room and pointed to the sectional couch. "This sectional couch doesn't pull out, but you can shape it into a bed if you like."

"I will be just fine, thank you so much for what you're doing. It means so much."

"Well, I've got a beer wondering why I've been gone so long. I'll see you later, just let me know if you need anything." Sam said as he walked out. "And don't worry about it. We all need a help up now and then."

"Thank you so much, Sam." She as she shut the door behind him as he staggered his way down the hall towards his own apartment.

Laura and Nick looked around in the apartment. Laura seemed very glad to have a place of her own to stay. She set the bag she was carrying down and said, "there's a layer of dust on everything."

Nick laughed, "it cleans up easy."

"Yeah, true." She said as walked over to the kitchen to check the drawers and see if there were any sponges, washcloths, or anything to use to clean the place up with.

She discovered a stack of kitchen towels and washcloths in one of the drawers.

"Perfect!" she said as she grabbed a washcloth out and wet under the sink faucet. She wrung it out and began wiping down the table and counter tops.

"I can show you around tomorrow if you'd like. There's a small market at the corner of the street and some other shops on the main street."

"That would be nice." she said without looking up as she continued to clean.

"Are you hungry? Would you like to come over to my apartment and have something to eat?"

"No,thank you. I already had something to eat with Nina before we got here. I just want to unpack my things and clean up this apartment a little."

"Say no more, I can take a hint. I'm going to head back to my apartment and get something to eat."

"Thanks for your help, Nick. I mean it. I'll come by later."

"If you need anything, I'll be next door at my place."

Nick left Laura's apartment and walked down the hallway to his which was the adjoining unit to hers.

He was still kind of in shock at all that had just taken place. He entered his apartment and just sulked a moment putting everything together in his head.

As he sat in the quiet thinking it over, he heard Laura

running the bathtub water next door through the wall from his apartment's bathroom.

Nick made himself a sandwich and grabbed a drink out of the refrigerator, before going into the living room to watch television. He could still hear the water running in the bathtub next door where Laura was when he left the kitchenette area.

After a bit, Nick heard the water turn off next door when he passed by the entryway to the bathroom next to the kitchen area. He smiled picturing Laura in his mind, naked and getting into the bathtub water. Not wanting to frustrate himself, he quickly tried to think of something else.

Nick went back into the living room to watch TV and keep my mind off such thoughts.

He watched television in the soft light that dimly illuminated the apartment from the street lights that were across the street. After a short while, he drifted off to sleep.

Nick woke up to a gentle knock on the door. At first he wasn't sure if he actually heard it or not. The knock was half in his dream before it actually woke him. He heard another soft knock on the door.

Nick sat up and got up to answer the door, stumbling in the dim light still half asleep. He unlocked the apartment door and opened it to see who it was.

To his delightful surprise, it was Laura. She was standing there with her hair nicely made up and he noticed that she also was wearing mascara. She stood there smiling at him as he stood there dumbfounded.

"Can I come in?" she said, breaking the awkward silence.

"Of course." Nick stepped back to let her come inside, closing it behind her.

This seemed weird to Nick because her hair was made up and she was wearing make-up, but she was wearing a light cotton nightgown and bobbi socks.

Additionally, there was the typical male observation that she wasn't wearing a bra either. Nick could see her nipples right through her nightgown in the light when she stepped past him coming inside his apartment. She also smelled very pretty and Nick found it erotic.

Laura sat down on the couch.

"Is it okay if I hang out here for a while?" she asked. "I don't have a TV or radio and it's pretty boring at my place."

"You're most welcome to stay as long as you like, can I get you something cold to drink?"

"Sure, what do you have?"

"My grand selection is limited to water, cola, or iced tea."

"I'll take a cola."

Nick went into the kitchenette and filled two glasses with ice and poured cold cola in them from the refrigerator. Nick brought their drinks and handed Laura hers while setting his down on a coaster on top of the coffee table.

Nick sat back down on the chair that was next to the couch. Laura took a sip from her drink and then set it down on a coaster on the coffee table next to his. She sat back in the couch and smiled at Nick.

"Why don't you come sit next to me?" she said as she patted the couch cushion next to her.

Nick smiled shyly and got up from his chair and sat down next to her on the couch. She took off her shoes and slid them under the coffee table and got more comfortable.

The room was dimly lit from the light emitting from the small television and the from the street lamps outside across the street. The lighting made Laura look even more enticing. She was, for lack of better words, beautiful beyond any comparison. Nick could smell her perfume, it was intoxicating and seducing him by scent alone. He loved the smell.

While her eyes were diverted watching television, Nick couldn't help but to look over and undress her with his eyes. He eyes followed her slender tanned neck and ran down past her soft shoulders to her breast line. He could see the soft suggestion of her breasts under her almost see-through cotton nightgown. When the light shifted from the TV, he could see the dark circles of her nipples through her nightgown. He couldn't help but notice that they were also poking out slightly through her nightgown.

His hand trembled slightly as his eyes continued to follow her body, past where her nightgown stopped and teasingly revealed her tanned thighs.

Nick tried to be casual and look back up at her eyes, he didn't want to be caught checking out her body. But as soon as he looked up at her eyes he seen that she'd been watching him admire her the whole time.

She smiled sweetly at him as his face started to blush from the instant embarrassment. He tried to look away, but she locked him in her eyes as she leaned forward while gently pulling him towards her.

She leaned the rest of the way forward and kissed him.

Nick nervously kissed her back. His inexperience made him awkward, especially when he felt her soft warm tongue enter his mouth. It startled him at first, he really didn't see any of this coming at all. Not that he wasn't glad for it.

He began to embrace her, dancing his tongue with hers in an increasing animalistic frenzy of lust.

She slid her hand up the back of his head, kissing him tighter as she placed his hand on her breast. She kept her hand over his preventing him from shyly pulling his hand away. He gently fondled while he reached the slender of her back with his other hand and embraced her in a deeply passionate kiss.

Laura gently pushed him back while looking down at the couch and asked, "does this pull out into a bed?"

She smiled at him flirtatiously and rubbed his chest while tugging at his shirt, making it quite clear why she asked.

"Yeah,..yeah it does." Nick said as he tried to wiggle up

from under her. She provocatively bit her lower lip and giggled as she stood up, pulling him up with her.

He pulled the couch cushions off and tossed them to the side of the couch near the wall. He turned towards her and gently pushed her back, momentarily pinning her against the wall as he kissed her.

Nick released her and took a step back before turning and taking hold of the strap in the middle of the couch and pulling out the hide-a-bed.

It was almost the size of a full size bed, although not nearly as comfortable. The mattress was thin and worn out. The support bars could be felt underneath it. Nick unfolded it all the way out into the bed position. It was already pre-made with a fitted sheet and a sheet tucked over it with a light blanket on top.

He put the bedding together earlier when he moved in after he bought a few groceries. He had a couple of pillows concealed behind the chairs which he grabbed and tossed on the bed.

"Oh, you have covers and pillows too," she said. "That's not fair, all I have is a blanket and a couch sectional thingy."

"Well you're of course most welcome to stay here in my bed with me as long and as much as you like." Nick said with a smile.

"If that would make you more comfortable," he added with a twinkle in his eye.

She smiled at him and climbed on the bed, pulling back

the sheet and blanket that were on top.

Nick just stood there and admired her as she moved cat-like on the bed., getting a flash of her backside as she climbed in and slid her legs under the sheets.

While Nick was scooting sideways along the bed, Laura reached under the sheet that she now had pulled up a little higher and began adjusting herself momentarily. A moment later she pulled her hand our from underneath the sheet and held her panties up in the air waving them at him.

Nick smiled at the sight of seeing her holding them up and nearly burst then. Her panties were soft pink and had a white lace that ran along the edges of them. They were erotic and more to the point, not on her anymore. Laura winked and smiled at him mischievously, tossing her panties on the floor.

After she had tossed her panties over the side of the bed, Nick pulled his t-shirt off and tossed it to the floor in front of the bed. He quickly laid down on top of the bed opposite of her. He was still wearing his shorts and was on top of the bed covers while she laid underneath them concealing her womanhood and all the glorious untold pleasures of her pure natural beauty.

She giggled at his shyness and said, "what are you doing way over there?"

Nick scooted towards her. His heart raced as he felt the loins of his shorts tighten and a wetness on the inside of his thigh.   He scooted beside her and whispered a soft gentle breath of hot air up her neck, gently caressing her shoulder softly with his lips as he moved across her neck then behind her ear. He kissed her ever so gingerly behind her ear as he glided his hand across her shoulder and up the side of her neck where he had just kissed. He could feel her squirm and softly groan with pleasure.

Nick could smell her hair and the perfume on her neck. Her aroma possessed him and aroused him with a greater desire for her than he ever had before.

Nick looked down into her soft eyes as she smiled back at him closing her eyes slightly and seductively as he bent down and kissed her ever so gently on the lips.

Laura reached up and grabbed the back of his head, pulling him down and kissed him hard, sliding her tongue back in his mouth animalistically. Her passion aroused him even further. She pulled him even tighter together as they kissed. Nick ran his hands up and down her back feeling the back of her cotton night shirt.

He felt the hard tips of her ladies as she brushed them against his chest. She also ran her hands along down his back to grab the belt line of his shorts and tug at them. Following his waist line, she slid her hands around front and felt for the zipper to his shorts.

Momentarily he was a little startled at her forward speed and without thinking he shyly pulled back a little.

Laura looked down at his crotch and unfastened the button of his shorts and then looked up into his eyes and whispered, "it's okay."

She began kissing him again as she unzipped his shorts. Once she got them open, she reached inside his underwear and grabbed him of by his manhood.

She pulled his shorts down as far as she could reach. Nick felt an almost uncontrollable lascivious passion metamorphose itself within him. A feeling he'd never felt before. Her seductive magnetism reached within him and drew out a passion that was hidden deep inside. It made him want her more than anything he'd ever wanted before. She held him tightly captive in her sensual spell as she reached in further and took ahold of him in a way he'd never been before.

Nick feared the levee would break before the rains even started. His body quivered from her deep passionate kiss. He struggled to maintain control, there was no way he was going to finish the dance when the music just started to play.

Nick manipulated his hands under her night shirt while feeling his way up past her ribs to her breasts. She took hold of his shoulders and pushed him back onto the bed, straddling him as he fondled her womanliness. She reached down crossing her arms at the bottom of her night shirt and then pulled it up over her head and off her body. She tossed it on the floor.

Still straddling him, she briefly held her hands behind her head to allow him to admire her voluptuous bosom in all its full glory. He beheld them as being more beautiful than he'd ever imagined they'd be. There were tan lines that ran around her breasts where she'd been tanning outside in the Sun most of the summer months. He could also see the tan lines where the bikini straps were. For some reason this made her breasts appear even more attractive to him.

Nick smiled when he looked into her eyes.

She brought her hands down and took hold of his, guiding them up her body to her breasts. He took hold of both of them with my hands and fondled them. They were smooth, soft and firm. As he brushed his thumbs across her hard erect nipples, she reached down and pulled his shorts the rest of the way off. She pulled pulled his underwear off with them at the same time. Tossing them to the floor beside the bed.

Nick laid there revealed and feeling vulnerably exposed with his soldier standing straight at attention with its helmet ready to be polished.

She seductively crawled catlike across the bed and moved over him, gently brushing his soldier with her breasts as she moved beside him. She laid partially across him with her leg straddling over his and began kissing him on the neck. She ran her hand over his chest and spread her fingers through his chest hair while he ran his hand down her body.

Nick moved his hand down across her tender backside and caressed her seat before I moving his hands up her back. He took her chin and brought her lips to his, kissing her passionately with a wolf's hunger that traveled through their entire bodies. Goosebumps formed on her tender skin and her whole body pulsed with her every breath.

Nick felt her wetness rub against his leg and this made his body quiver in desire for her. His manhood had a mind of its own and reached out to her. He took hold of her and kissed her down her body. He could feel her body melt in his hands as he worked his way down to her secret garden.

Leaving her to float adrift in a cloud of ecstasy. She swooned in pleasure arching her back as he greedily devoured every ounce of passion she had and left her in an euphoric state.

While she was still glossy eyed and ecstatically trembling, he moved up to her side and laid beside her. Embracing her in sweet loving comfort as they both drifted off to sleep.

Chapter 13

Nick woke up the next morning and immediately noticed that he was laying in bed alone. He was still nude under the blanket and he never slept that way. It made him feel uncomfortable. He sat up in the bed and looked around the room and into the kitchen area for Laura. He didn't see her. He listened for a moment to see if maybe if could hear if she was in the bathroom.

The television was still on, but the volume was on low and there was just static in the screen. It had served as a night light more than anything. Nick crawled to the end of the bed to reach over and turn it off. It was still a little dark in the room, the curtains were still drawn from last night.

However, Nick didn't recall closing the curtains last night. In fact, he distinctly remembered the street light outside lighting the room last night. Perhaps Laura closed them during the night or this morning.

He got out of bed and sought out his shorts and underwear that were on the floor. He put them on and walked in the kitchenette area to see if Laura was in the bathroom. The bathroom door was open and the light was off. He walked into the bathroom, turned the light on and used the toilet.

'She must have got up while I was still asleep and left for her apartment next door.'

He stood there briefly and listened at the bathroom wall to see if he could hear her next door. It was silent.

Nick turned off the bathroom light and went back in the living room where he opened the window curtains and lit up the apartment. He looked around the apartment for evidence of Laura. Her shoes and clothes were gone. But of course, she probably gathered them up and dressed before going back to her place.

Nick pulled the bed sheets up and made the bed. As he was making up the bed he could see the imprint on the mattress of where she had laid.

He smiled reflecting back on last night. He tucked the sheets and blanket in and then folded up the bed, turning it into a couch once again. He pulled the coffee table back into place and transformed the bed chamber back into a living room again. The drink glasses they used last night were still set on the coasters on the coffee table. The ice had long melted and diluted their drinks, leaving behind water marks on the coasters. Nick grabbed both glasses and carried them into the kitchen, dumping the contents out into the sink drain.

Nick walked back into the living room and sat on the couch momentarily replaying the night again in his head. He was giddy and happier than he'd been in a long time.

214

He wanted to go to her, but wondered why she just up and left without saying a word. Looking at the time, he decided that it wouldn't be too early to go over there. First he went into the bathroom to clean up and brush his hair. He also brushed his teeth and put on some cologne. He wanted to be nice looking and smelling fresh when he met with her. Adjusting his clothes, he inspected himself one last time in the mirror before leaving and walking down the hall to Laura's apartment.

He knocked on Laura's door and stood there a moment listening for a response. Hearing anything, he knocked again, this time a little louder. Again he stood there and listened. Still nothing, it was quiet.

'She must be a heavy sleeper,' he thought.

Nick reached up and knocked again. He felt a little guilty for knocking again and not coming back later to let her sleep a little longer. But he wanted to see her, he *had* to see her. He'd always felt something for her, but always put it behind in my mind because she was Steve's girlfriend. But now she was with him and he definitely felt something very strong for her now.

He wanted to embrace her and tell her the truth about how he felt about her. He knocked on the door again a little more persistent than before. As he grew more impatient, he anxiously began to shift his weight from side to side.

'She had to hear me knocking at this point.'

Nick knocked again while feeling his heart sink a little because she wasn't answering.

Nick stood in front of her door pondering where she might be when the door across the hall opened. It was the old man who lived there.

"Nobody lives there, you should know that!" he barked at Nick. "Why the hell do you keep pounding on that door for anyways? I'm trying to sleep!"

After giving Nick one final scald, the old man grumpily slammed his apartment door shut.

Nick just stood there stunned looking at the old man's closed door. He didn't mean to bother the old man, but damn. The senile old bugger wasn't even aware that the apartment had been rented last night.

He looked at the door knob to Laura's apartment and considered trying it to see if it was unlocked or not. Perhaps he could maybe go in and wake her up. But then he thought better of that because it would be a violation of trust just walking in uninvited.

Nick walked back to his apartment and shut the door behind him. He decided to wait a bit and try again later. He didn't know how she was feeling or anything. He knew Steve had planned to break up with her, but he didn't think it would happen later that day. By the way he was talking, Nick assumed that it was going to happen in a couple of weeks or so. He could only imagine what emotional turmoil she must be going through. She probably wanted to be left alone for a bit and didn't want to see or talk to anyone.

Nick knew it would be best to wait perhaps until at least after lunch if she didn't already come over. She could have also got up to walk around and check out the local shops or get some groceries. He would just have to wait a bit and try to keep her off his mind by watching TV or something.

He walked over and turned on the television set then sat on the couch and tried to drone out the many thoughts flying through his mind. Unfortunately, it wasn't working. He could still smell her sweet perfume in the air from last night.

Chapter 14

Nick spent much of the morning cleaning up his apartment. He had a mop to clean the kitchenette and bathroom floors but he didn't have a vacuum cleaner for the worn out musty smelling carpet. He only had a broom that was left in the apartment, so he swept the carpet as best he could; spraying it with air freshener to mask the putrid moldy dirt smell. He also pounded the dust out of the couch cushions and then sprayed them with air fresher too.

Nick's apartment now mostly smelled of floral air freshener. He wasn't sure what was worse, the musty smell or the floral air freshener smell. He opened a couple of windows to air out some of the excessive smell of the aerosol he sprayed on everything.

A couple of hours had passed and he still heard nothing next door.

Now bored, he decided to go and see what Joe was doing. He was sure that while he was in the middle of cleaning his apartment that he heard Joe's apartment door open and close a few times.

Nick walked down the hall to Joe's and knocked on his door.

"It's unlocked! Come in!" Nick heard Joe yell from the other side of the door.

Nick opened the door and entered the apartment. He seen Joe sitting on a chair across the room with his feet kicked up on the ledge of an opened window. It was warm outside today and the old apartment complex didn't have any air conditioning in any shape or form. The only way to stay cool in the apartments was by means of assorted fans, open windows and, of course to be armed with a fly swatter.

Joe was hanging back in a chair reading a book with his shirt unbuttoned, wearing shorts, and hanging his bare feet out the window. Joe was a science fiction junkie and would almost always have a science fiction book near him somewhere. Space stories were the ones that interested him the most.

"Hey! How's it going?" greeted Nick as he shut the door behind him.

"I'm just sitting around reading and trying not to melt in the heat. First it's cold, then it's humid. I don't think the weather really knows what it wants to do."

"Oh yeah, I have the windows in my apartment open too."

"You're just in time" Joe said, "I was ready to take a break."

"Oh? What did I make it just in time for?" joked Nick.

Smiling with a big cheesy grin, Joe pulled out a joint from his shirt pocket.

"Do you wanna come smoke it with me?"

"Who am I to turn down an offer like that?" Nick jested.

Joe laughed and put it back in his shirt pocket.

"My mom may be coming over this afternoon so we have to smoke it elsewhere."

"We can always go to mine." Nick offered.

Joe shook his head "no, I have a better idea."

He closed his book, got up from the chair and walked over to the apartment door and motioned Nick to follow him.

"Come on, I'll show you a nice cool place."

Nick followed Joe out of the apartment and shut the door behind him.

"Don't worry about locking it, nobody's going to mess with it around here." Joe said as he walked down the corridor.

Nick quickly caught up and followed behind him. Nick wasn't sure where they were going, but he was confident that wherever it was that it wouldn't be too far. After all, Joe didn't put any shoes on and you just didn't walk around in "the hood" without any shoes on. It was a good way to slice your foot open.

Joe stopped halfway down the hallway just before the door to Nick's apartment and pointed up.

"See up there?" he said, looking upwards.

Nick looked up and nodded. There was a huge ventilation hole in the ceiling with a big fan in it.

"The fan motor is burnt out. It's suppose to vent out some of the hot air or it can change directions and pull in cooler air from the outside," he explained.

"So?" Nick mocked. "Is there where you keep the dead bodies?"

"Oh, ha ha. Hey, I wouldn't joke about stuff like that. I was watching the news this morning and they found some old lady's dead body in the cemetery.

"Well, where else are you going to find dead old ladies?" Nick said as he started to laugh at his own joke.

Joe laughed. "No seriously, it wasn't a buried body, someone just dumped it there or something."

"Oh. So what's the deal with this fan?"

"It leads up to the roof," Joe said with a big smile on his face.

"First you jump up and grab that bar there." He pointed up towards the bar in the middle of the passageway up. Nick looked up and seen what he was pointing and nodded.

"Then you pull yourself up and go up past the fan. Make sure that it's off though, just in case," he said, pointing to a switch near the opening.

"Just pull yourself up, stand on the bar and crawl past the fan to that vent door. It just swings out. There's a spring on it that pulls it back shut."

Nick looked up and took it all in for a moment.

"Okay." Nick said with a nod. "Let's do this."

Joe stood under the ventilation hole and looked up for a moment before jumping and grabbing the metal bar. Nick stood back and watched him climb his way up, paying close attention to what he was doing. Joe crawled up through the hole in the vent and pulled himself up past the vent fan and then through the vent door.

"Come on." he said, poking his head in through the vent door.

Nick jumped up and tried to grab the bar, but missed it by a few inches. He was a little shorter than Joe and obviously needed put a little more effort in jumping. He jumped again, a little higher this time and almost grabbed the bar. He hit his finger on the bar and jammed it when he tried to grab it. The pain shot up his finger and began to throb.

"Sonofabitch!" Nick exclaimed, grabbing hold of his injured finger and did a short dance of pain around on the floor .

'Great', he thought. 'just what I need now is to break my fingers.'

He inspected his finger and tried to bend it. All fingers

bent and didn't really hurt as much after a minute.

Nick looked up at the bar again and positioned himself under it. This time when he leapt up he successfully grabbed the bar with both hands. Nick pulled himself u while looking at the fan nervously.

"I hope as hell, he's right about it not working,"

The fan had large metal blades with a rather large motor attached to it. He wasn't sure if it would slice a person in half or not, but he wasn't going to test whether or not it could. He pulled himself up to the ledge that was just above the fan and stood on the bar. Steadying himself, he pushed the vent door open and pulled himself up the rest of the way through, joining Joe on the rooftop.

The trees around the building had grown higher than the building and shaded it from the midday's scorching sun. Remarkably, the roof was actually slightly cooler than it was downstairs by a few degrees. The trees allowed a slight breeze through to help cool the rooftop. The trees that encircled the rooftop blocked out the rest of the surrounding world as best as trees could do within city limits.

Joe was sitting down on the roof with his back to the side of the vent fixture. It was about the size of a dog house, except that it was square. Nick sat next to him.

"Be careful sitting down. This black roof is dirty and will leave dirt and black marks on ya if you're not careful."

Nick carefully sat down, trying not to smug his pants as Joe pulled the joint out of his pocket and lit it up. He took a deep hit from it and then passed it to Nick, who also took a large hit and passed it back.

They passed it back of forth between themselves in this manner for a few minutes until Joe finally asked, "why do you smell so pretty?"

Nick laughed at his question. Perhaps he was a little high at this point, but he still thought it was funny for him to ask him that.

"Laura showed up last night and spent the night with me."

"Oh, congratulations dude." Joe mocked. "But I'm not sure who Laura is or whether or not I've met her. Is she hot?"

"You remember your old girlfriend, Nina?"

Joe nodded.

"She used to be Nina's old roommate until she started dating Steve."

"Ah ya, I know who you're talking about now."

"She showed up last night needing a place to stay, she and Steve broke up."

"Dude, I don't know who Steve is."

"Well, no matter, he's gone now."

"It's cool, I get it. She was dating this dude, they broke up and there she is at your door. Right?"

"Yeah, pretty much. She came over with her stuff in

hand and needed somewhere to stay. Like I did when I showed up at your door."

"Hey, don't worry about that dude, everyone goes through a pinch in life."

"Yeah, and don't get me wrong, I wanted her to stay....like bad."

Joe laughed. "I get it dude, hahaha!"

"Yeah, but when she was outside my door about to carry her stuff in, your uncle showed up."

Joe looked at him oddly. "What do you mean?"

"He heard her in the hallway and just came out to see who it was."

Joe nodded.

"But then he gave her the apartment on the end to rent, with the same deal like he did me."

Joe piped in, "oh really? There wasn't anyone in it this morning when I went in to make sure the refrigerator was unplugged."

Nick gave him a puzzled look.

"I'm suppose to keep everything turned off and unplugged until someone rents it," he said. "I had that one plugged in yesterday to make sure the freezer on it still worked."

"The apartment on the end?"

"Yeah. I went in to check it this morning before

226

unplugging it."

"You sure? Because he rented that end apartment to Laura last night. She's got her stuff in there."

"I didn't notice anybody's stuff down there. But I was trying to hurry and didn't really look around. I just went in, made sure the freezer was cold and unplugged it."

"I don't think we're talking about the same unit. The one across from the old guy."

"Yeah. I left the door unlocked if you want to check."

They heard a car pull up into the parking lot below.

Joe stood up, dusting his pants off and said, "that's my mom, I knew she'd probably show up today."

"I have to go, I'll see ya later." he said as he headed towards the vent they crawled up through.

He climbed through the vent door and lowered himself down to the bar past the fan and then hung on the bar just before dropping down on the hallway floor down below. Nick watched him climb down, so he'd know how to get back down off the rooftop.

Before walking off, Joe hollered up the vent at Nick and said, "don't bust your ass coming down."

Joe laughed at his own remark as he walked away towards his apartment, trying to get there before his mother came up the front door stairs that were just around the corner from his apartment.

Nick sat on the roof for a few moments and enjoyed the

cool shade. He was curious about Laura. Joe said the door was probably unlocked and that he'd been in there earlier that morning. But Nick was sure he was talking about the wrong apartment.

Nick got up from where he was sitting and carefully climbed through the vent door, trying not to get dirty in doing do. He scooted into position so he could lower himself past the fan and down to the bar below it. He climbed down and swung himself onto the bar. Hanging down, he let go and dropped down to the carpeted hallway below.

When he landed, he clumsily stumbled and went down to his knees, flopping forward and nearly landing on his face.

'I really don't think I'm going to go up there anymore unless I have to.'

Nick got up off the floor and walked into his apartment. Now he had to clean back up a little before he went over and seen if Laura was back yet. He didn't want to look all dirty from being on the roof nor did he want to smell like weed either.

Nick went into the bathroom and washed his hands in the bathroom sink. He inspected himself to make sure he didn't get his clothes dirty and brushed his hair again. A final touch of spraying a little more cologne to cover up the weed smell and he was satisfied that he was presentable once again for Laura.

He shut off the bathroom light and walked around into

the living room to leave his apartment and see if Laura was home.

He walked down the hallway to Laura's apartment door and again knocked on it as he'd done earlier that day. He didn't knock very loud though; he didn't want to bother the cantankerous old man across the hall.

After waiting for about a minute or so and hearing no answer, he reached down and tried the door handle. It wasn't locked, so he opened the apartment door.

Slowly Nick pushed open the door and called in, "hello?! Laura? Is anyone here?"

There wasn't an answer, so he pushed the door open even further and called out again, "hello? Laura, are you here? It's Nick."

Poking his head in the partially opened doorway, Nick listened for any kind of response. He didn't hear anyone so he pushed the apartment door open the rest of the way and went inside.

"Hello. Is anyone here?"

He walked into the living area and looked around for any sign of Laura. He didn't see her and there didn't seem to be anything of hers in the living room.

Cautiously he walked into the kitchenette, calling out before going in.

"Hello, are you there?"

He noticed that the counters were empty and dusty,

which was odd because he remembered seeing her wipe them down last night before he left. He remembered watching her wipe the kitchen table clean too, because he caught a glimpse of her cleavage when she was bent over wiping it.

The refrigerator was pulled away from the wall and unplugged with its door open with a single open box of baking soda set on one of the refrigerator's shelves.

"That's odd. Maybe Joe did come in here this morning and unplug that."

The bathroom was empty too. There weren't any of her bags, clothes, or anything.

He turned around and looked around in the apartment again. There was absolutely no sign of Laura or her things in the entire apartment at all. The apartment was empty and abandoned. Nobody was here and there wasn't any sign of anyone lived in it for quite a while. There was a dust film over everything, it was obvious that nobody had been in there for a long time.

'Where the hell could she be if she wasn't here? Maybe she left last night or early this morning when she left my apartment while I was still asleep.'

Nick's heart sank with the thought of her leaving without a word. He hoped that maybe she'd left a note or something and looked around the apartment one last time before leaving.

Empty handed, he shut the apartment door behind him and walked down the hall back to his apartment.

230

Just as he reached the door to his apartment, the apartment manager's door opened and Sam came out.

Sam waved and said, 'hello.'

Nick waved back and tried to get in his apartment.

"How'd ya sleep last night? Was the apartment comfortable?" Sam asked as he walked towards Nick.

"Great! Thank you! Hey, do you know if Laura moved out or not?"

Sam gave him a puzzled look. "Who's Laura?"

"That girl who showed up here last night. You rented her the corner apartment."

"Sorry, nobody named Laura has come around. I haven't rented that corner apartment in a while. We just now got the water working in it."

Nick was puzzled.

"But if Laura or anyone else shows up looking for an apartment to rent, let them know that it's for rent."

Sam turned and walked down the hall to the stairs outside.

'That was certainly strange as hell,' he thought.

Nick didn't trust Sam's memory, after all he was a bit of a daily drunk and probably didn't even remember renting it to her anyways. He reassured himself that Laura had indeed been there last night as he went back into his apartment and shut the door behind him.

After sitting in the quiet of his apartment for a while, he reasoned that she'd probably just bailed in the night after he fell asleep and simple nobody remembered her even being there. Except for him of course.

It was a night he'd never forget.

The part that bothered him the most was that she probably just slipped out the door and quietly went to her apartment, grabbed her bags and slipped out without looking back. It made him feel horrible that she'd leave without saying a word or even leaving a note behind.

To just disappear in the night like a dream.

His eyes warmed and grew teary His emotions took a serious plunge when he resolved what she most likely had done. The realization that she probably slipped out in the night without so much as a word. It made tore at his heart.

Nick slumped in his chair, feeling physically drained and empty. He just stared in the direction of the wall at nothing. He fell into his own mental world as his mind raced through a series of emotions.

Mostly feeling sorry for himself because he was heartbroken.

'What was wrong with me? Why did she just leave me like that. She wouldn't even give me a chance or the common courtesy of a friend to say a simple 'goodbye.' Playing with my emotions like that. To come to me and seize my heart and then just as quickly, vanish away in the night while I slept. Making the whole thing all seem as if it were nothing more than a dream.'

He couldn't just lose her like that. Not without a
fighting chance. He had to find her. He had to figure out
where she slipped off to and why. He couldn't just let it go
like that.

Considering the most probably places she'd be, he
figured that she'd most likely be at Nina's place. Nina had
dropped her off at his apartment last night and most likely
would be the person to come pick her up.

Nick reached into his back pocket and pulled out his
wallet. He dug out a folded notebook sheet which he kept
phone numbers written down on. He scanned the list and
found Nina's telephone number and decided to walk down
to the corner market and use the pay phone they had.

Nick wiped the tears that were starting to form and
recomposed himself. He left his apartment, locking the
door behind him and walked down the hallway to leave.
He paused momentarily by the door that was Laura's
apartment before heading outside and walking to the
corner market, which was only a couple of blocks up the
street.

He walked briskly and arrived at the corner market, a
small convenience store which had bars on the windows
and cameras in every direction. He walked up to one of the
pay phones hanging on the wall just around the corner of
the market's front door. He inserted his coins and dialed
Nina's number.

It rang a few times before Nina finally answered in a
groggy voice. It was Saturday and she was probably trying
to sleep off Friday's late night party.

"Hello, Nina? This is Nick. Did I wake you?"

"Hello. Yes, you did wake me up, but that's alright I have to get up anyways."

"I'm sorry for waking you up."

"Don't worry about it, it's okay. Why'd ya call? What do you want?"

"I was wanting to know if Laura was there or not. Is she?"

"No, she's not here bud. I haven't her since the other day when we were at the pool."

"But didn't you give her a ride to my place last night?"

"Huh-uh. Not me, I don't even know where you live. I haven't seen her. I've been at home all night partying. Some friends came over, some of who are still passed out on her floor, but not Laura. Why? What's the matter?"

"Oh, nothing's the matter. I was just looking for her and thought she maybe came by your place."

"Sorry bud. I haven't seen her."

"That's cool. Thanks anyways."

"No problem. I don't mean to cut this short, but I gotta get ready for work."

"Okay then, I'll talk to you another time. Thanks Nina!"

Nick said goodbye and hung up the phone. He heard the coins he put in the pay telephone drop inside as he did.

Nick called a couple of other numbers where he felt

Laura may have also gone. None of them had seen or heard from her recently.

Unable to locate her, he walked back to his apartment. But before he went back to his own apartment, he stopped at the corner apartment and opened the door to look through it one last time. It was still unlocked.

He entered the apartment to look one last time to put his mind at ease.

The apartment was well lit up from all the shades being drawn open. He could see the dust floating in the air as he walked into the kitchenette area and looked around. The counter top and everything else in there was coated with a film of dust. He turned and looked down at the kitchen table top. It was smudged and coated with dust as well.

He could have sworn seeing her set her bags on the floor next to the table and grabbing a rag out of the kitchen drawer, wetting it in the sink and then wiping the table clean. He remembered asking her if she was hungry and if she wanted to come over and get something to eat.

The sink had a film of dust in it. It apparently hadn't been turned on in quite a while.

He walked over and pulled the kitchen drawer open and seen that there were a couple of rags and washcloths in there.

'That was where Laura got the one she used to clean with. How else would I have known exactly which kitchen drawer to open and find the washcloths?'

The washcloth on top looked like the one she used to clean with. It was laying there in the drawer, untouched and dusty from being in the drawer so long. The whole apartment was very dusty.

He walked into the bathroom and looked down at the bathtub. He remembered hearing her take a bath last night. He sat down on the edge of the bathtub and reached over to turn the water on. Nothing came out.

He turned the knob all the way and still no water came out. He tried twisting the knob the other way and still no water. '

'What the hell?'

Nick stood up and reached over to turn the faucet knobs in the sink on.

"There's no water in this apartment right now." he heard said behind him.

Startled, he nearly jumped out of his skin and turned around to see Sam standing there looking at him, holding a beer in his hand.

"Whoa! You spooked me." Nick said while grabbing his chest. "I didn't hear you come in."

Sam laughed aloud and then took a huge swig from the can of beer he was holding.

After letting out a long beer induced belch, he pointed to the bathtub with his beer and said, "the faucet's busted in that bathtub, *<belch>* luckily it only sprayed water in the bathtub when it busted off and didn't ruin the floor."

He took another swig from his beer and continued, "I don't know how in the hell they broke it off, but the folks that lived here before said that it just blew off when they used it. Personally, I call bullshit on that one because faucets don't just bust off."

His drunken accent was kind of hard for Nick to understand, so he just nodded.

"Anyways, I had to shut the water off to this apartment to fix it. I just haven't turned the water back on yet because nobody's rented it yet."

He looked at Nick and asked, "were ya thinking about switching to this apartment? I can turn the water back on real quick, if ya want. It only takes a moment for me to go down to the ground floor and turn it back on."

"Well, I was just looking at it, but I think I'll keep the one I've got right now." Nick lied. He didn't want him to know that he was snooping around the apartment to see if he could find any hint of Laura being there.

Sam then turned to walk out. "Just let me know if you decide to switch apartments and I'll turn the water on in it."

"Thanks, but I think I'll just keep the apart,ent I have."

Nick left the apartment with Sam, shutting the door behind him and went into his own apartment while Sam continued walking towards his apartment, taking finishing chugs of his beer.

Nick sat down on the couch.

He wasn't sure what to think about it all of this. Could

it all have possibly been just a dream? It seemed real enough that she'd been here. He began to doubt himself as to whether or not it all really happened. He seemed to be the only one on Earth that thought she was there last night.

He looked down at the coffee table in front of him and noticed the two beverage coasters they used last night. Both of the drinking coasters still had water stains on them from the drinks that were sat on them all night. The water stains were dried up but still visible on the cork coasters.

He got up and looked in the kitchen by the sink and seen the two drinking glasses from last night. One of them was his and the other was Laura's drink.

'She was here.'

He could even faintly still smell her perfume in the air. It was almost gone thanks to his spraying air freshener everywhere, but he could still faintly smell it.

Frustrated, Nick pulled the couch cushions off and pulled the bed out. In his haste, he nearly hit the coffee table behind him when he forgot to move it out of the way. Moving the table out of the way, he pulled the hide-a-bed the rest of the way out and crawled on it to pull the covers back. He bent down to smell the sheet and it smelled strongly of her perfume.

'She was here. I knew I wasn't crazy or that it was just a dream.'

He got off the bed and put the covers back where they were and sat on the edge of the bed. His heart sank deeper with the thought of her sneaking out while he slept, leaving no trace behind.

'What the hell was that all about? What did I do to make her sneak off in the night like that?'

Nobody else seemed to remember Laura being there either. He rationalized that Sam was drunk almost all his waking moment and always had a beer in his hand. So he could understand why Sam couldn't remember Laura being there and renting her an apartment. After all, chances are that Sam was probably drunk and doesn't even remember what he had for breakfast this morning.

But Nina not remembering dropping her off here last night or seeing and waving at him was very strange. Nina said she didn't even know where he lived. But, she could also be lying for Laura. He had to consider that.

He was really baffled by it all and starting to question everything. Was it all an illusion and not real?

He had to find her and verify this himself. He was now so unsure of himself and what was real or not. He couldn't even think straight anymore.

Nick was hurt and confused.

Chapter 15

Nick spent most of the weekend calling just about everyone he could think of trying to find Laura without the slightest bit of success. He did verify that Steve had in fact moved back to his home state from someone that helped him pack up when he left. He also verified through a friend that Steve and Laura did break up and that she didn't leave with him. It was also confirmed by another friend that Steve was alone when he left for his home state.

Nick speculated that there was always that chance that Laura could have called Steve and he in turn could have picked her up as he drove out of town, taking her with him. But the likelihood of that was null, because Steve had left that afternoon on the same day that Laura had shown up later in that same evening. The possibility of her leaving with Steve was pretty much eliminated as he was already gone and out of the state.

Either way, she was nowhere to be found and had left without a trace. Where she'd gone, nobody knew. Everyone that Nick contacted had not seen or heard from her. Nonetheless, he had to get on with his life. This was heart breaking, but not the end of the World.

Nick resolved that he had to stick with the plan he had before she even showed up. He didn't even expect her to be there in the first place and in all truth, never really expected to ever see her again prior to that. So her being equated into his plans didn't even exist in the first place.

'I mustn't think of this as being anything more than a pleasant surprise that's come and gone. Nothing more.'

His current needs were to find a job so he could pay the rent and improve upon his life's situation. It was hindering that he didn't have a phone or car. This would make finding a job more difficult. But he was determined he'd find a way to make things work out through pure determination and maintaining self confidence.

Raw determined perseverance will path the way to success.

His current situation was that of an affordable yet barely tolerable apartment. That was about all it amounted to in all honesty. It was definitely better than living on the streets. He was optimistic that things could only improve from here on after.

He'd spent much of remainder of the week filing out employment applications with no real immediate success. He spent much of his time moping about in his apartment. Now and then, he stare at the corner apartment and wonder about Laura. He just couldn't shake her from his mind. At this point, he accepted the probability that she had not really been here.

There was also something that he couldn't quite explain. But he felt that everything happening probably had something to do with that stupid ceramic idol he smashed. After all, a whole chain of unexplainable events immediately followed. All of which led to him being there in that apartment in the first place.

Out of pure boredom, Nick wandered into the vacant apartment that was across the hall from his apartment. He looked at when he first arrived and chose which apartment he wanted. It was the one that really didn't have any furniture in it.

He had no idea why he wandered in there. More or less for something to do, just to poke around. It was just a dirty apartment with dust all over the place. The refrigerator was unplugged and pulled away from the wall. There wasn't a box of baking soda in this one like there was in all the other apartments.

The open unclean refrigerator left a sour mildew smell that seemed to linger in the air.

Nick walked over to the center of the living room and sat on the floor in the dark empty apartment. For no reason, he just sat down cross-legged and stared down at the floor, thinking about nothing. Just dull and blank-minded.

The room was dimly lit from the street light outside that beamed in past the trees and through the shadeless old windows. He wasn't in total darkness, but it was darker in there now than it was when he'd first went in there.

He must have been sitting there staring at the floor longer than he thought, but he really couldn't tell how long it had been. It was early in the evening with the sun still up when he entered the empty apartment. It just got dark quickly while he sat there on the floor.

Coming to his senses, he looked around in the room and realized that he had to snap out of this mopiness. After all, what was he doing in this empty apartment just sitting there in the dark. Normally he prevented going into dark places, yet there he was.

Looking around he noticed something in the corner of the room. It was getting darker in the room so it was hard to tell what it was. It was just setting there on the floor.

Nick stood up from his sitting position on the floor. His legs ached and tingled as if a million little needles were poking them. His legs had fallen asleep from sitting there too long cross legged. He shook his legs a little to get the blood flowing in them again and walked over to see what was on the floor.

It was some sort of book.

This was great, he could use something to read. He hoped it was a good book, something worth reading. He picked up the book up, but it was too dark to really see what the title or anything was. Nick walked towards the center of the room to take a look at it in the light coming through the windows.

He suddenly felt very uncomfortable. He looked up and noticed that the shadows on the walls and ceiling were beginning to creep their way towards him from the corners of the room. They were literally pushing out the light ahead of them.

He felt the coldness of something in the room. It no longer felt like he was alone in there.

'Something's in the room with me.'

He couldn't see it, but he could definitely feel it. He felt its eyes on him and it made his skin crawl. He tried to shake off the feeling and not look over his shoulders. Pretending he didn't notice the presence in the shadows, he looked back down at the book.

The book was really old. It was bound in leather and the pages were a bit odd, because they were thick. He'd never seen book pages like this before. It was like they were made from something different from regular paper. They were yellowed and there were watermarks all over it, which made the pages kind of wavy and brittle.

Nick carefully turned the pages and seen that the first few pages were blank. He could see tear marks near the bottom inside the binding where some of the front pages had been torn out. He flipped through a few more pages and seen that rest of the pages had writing on them. Fancy hand writing, not printed. He could tell that the book itself had been made and written by hand.

It looked like it was written with a calligraphy pen.

Even though Nick recognized how it was written, he didn't recognize the letters or alphabet that the book was written in. It looked like it was written some other language or something that used an alphabet he's never seen before. Several of the pages were written in this odd alphabet with symbols and diagrams drawn here and there. By the symbol drawings there was writing in the form of notes. Some pages looked like they were lists, as if they were recipes. Those pages looked like a list of ingredients or something.   Most of the other pages seemed like they were notes or something. He really couldn't tell, he couldn't understand a single word that was written in it.

He was careful thumbing through the dusty old book as to not tear any of its fragile pages. The handwriting stopped for a few pages and were blank. Near one of the last pages, there was handwriting in Latin characters and in English. It read:

Defray Charon's conveyance, perdition hath;

Empyrean weregilds perfidies, avarice, and wrath.

Alight the underzeal to Ganga's midnight.

Temperance lustrates the desecrations forbate;

Heaved beyond Firmament will the Premier allocate.

Nick stared blankly at the writing for a moment and blinked his eyes several times. He looked at it and reread it several more times.

"Oh my god, I'm going to have to get a dictionary just to read this. I don't even know or understand half of these words."

Nick felt that there must have some kind of obvious underlining meaning that he just wasn't getting. He could tell that it was written in the same handwriting as the rest of the book.

It suddenly dawned on him about the darkness that had been slowly encroaching all around him. He'd become so sidetracked with his curiosity about finding the dusty old book that he wasn't even paying attention.

He also ignored the growing feeling that some kind of presence was in the room with him. He looked up and all he could see was darkness around him. Even stranger was that it wasn't dark immediately around him. He could see the book and the writing in it. He could even see a couple of feet around him. But everywhere else was nothing but blackness.

Oddly enough, he wasn't afraid or even alarmed. Normally, he'd been petrified in fear to be in such darkness, especially weird unexplainable darkness creeping from nowhere. He always felt an immense dread while in the darkness, but not now for some reason. He felt safe in his little aura of light that seemed to strangely be around him, keeping the darkness back. But only safe in the strange aura of light around him.

He also became aware of the presence that was still hiding in the shadows.

Yes, the presence. He felt it when the darkness began to creep in from every direction around him. Just before he noticed the strange book in the corner of the floor. He felt it alright and it felt like there were many of them, not just one presence. He could feel their eyes on him from all around, watching him. There was another strange feeling he had. He could actually feel their hatred.

Even though Nick felt safe in the strange light around him, he felt afraid to step out it. He had no idea where this illumination around him came from, but he was glad it was there. It wasn't very bright, but there wasn't any light above him, he could see the ceiling.

'Is this book causing this?

He had a very weird feeling about the book and its strange writings and symbols. Without even thinking, he tossed it on the ground, in the darkness.

The book hit the ground ahead of him in the darkness with a solid thump. Just as it did, both the illumination and the darkness that drowned out the world around him disappeared in an instant.

It was one of the strangest things Nick had ever seen in his life.

The room was still darkened a bit, but not pitch black as it had been before with the light aura. The empty apartment was once again partially lit up from the outside street lights that beamed in through the windows. Nick felt now would be a great time to get out of there.

He looked down at the book he tossed on the floor.

'What was this thing?'

Nick walked over to the door and opened it. He squinted as the light from the hallway momentarily blinded him. He stepped into the hallway for a moment and allowed his eyes to adjust to the light. Once his eyes cleared, he looked into the empty apartment again. It was dark in there, but a normal dark with the illumination from the outside lights. There were the usual shadows in the corners.

He felt it again. That feeling as if something was watching him from the darkness. He looked down on the floor and seen the dusty old book. He wasn't sure if he really wanted to step back in there again. But he felt he needed to retrieve the book.

Not understanding exactly why, but he felt he needed that book. He felt as if he somehow didn't find it as much as it found him.

He felt like he was suppose to find this book.

Feeling a bit cowardly, he stood in the doorway looking at the book on the floor inside the apartment from the safety of the hallway and its light. He had to go back in there and get it, but it seemed like the shadows in the corners were daring him to come in. Waiting for him walk back in and then lunge at him the very second he tried.

'This is nonsense.'

Growing impatient with himself, Nick stormed into the apartment and deliberately marched into the center of the living room where the book was setting on the floor. He bent down and picked it up, then quickly turned right back around and headed toward the door. He could still feel the unseen eyes on him, but that wasn't going to slow him down one bit. He went out the door and was back in the hallway with the book securely in his hand.

He turned around to close the door to the dark empty

apartment and as soon as he reached for doorknob it slammed shut in his face. Nick felt the rush of air blow past him when it slammed shut.

He heard a door open down the hall. It was Joe.

"Hey! Is everything alright?"

"Yeah, everything's okay."

Joe started walking down the hallway towards Nick.

"What was that loud boom?"

"Sorry about that, the wind slammed the door shut."

"Be careful about that. You don't want to disturb the other tenants."

"Yeah, sorry about that."

"What you been up to lately?"

"No much really. Still haven't had any luck finding a job yet."

Noticing the book Nick was holding he asked, "what's that?"

At this point Nick wasn't really sure how to answer. He wasn't doing anything wrong. Joe was the one that told him that it was okay to go into the abandoned apartments. He said nobody cared and if there was anything in them that he wanted for his apartment, he was welcome to go and get it. Nick figured that Joe probably knew about this book. Maybe it was his.

Nick held up the book and said, "I found this book in

250

that abandoned apartment."

"Oh wow, really? Can I see it?"

"Sure." Nick handed it to him.

Joe took the book and looked at it, flipping through the pages. After a moment he asked, "you found this in one of the empty apartments?"

"Yeah," said Nick as pointed to the apartment across the hall.

Joe nodded and said, "huh,.. I've been in that apartment quite a few times and I've never seen it in there before."

"Really? It was in the living room sitting on the floor in the corner."

"Strange. I never noticed it before."

He closed the book, shrugged his shoulders and handed it back to Nick, who took the book and opened his apartment door.

"Do you want to come in?"

"Naw, thanks. I'm tired. I was about to go to bed when I heard the door slam. But I'll probably see ya tomorrow though. Come over tomorrow when you get up." he said as walked back down to his apartment.

Nick went into his apartment and set the book down on the coffee table, feeling uneasy. He turned on every light int he apartment before settling down on the couch for the night. He didn't bother pulling the bed out and just slept on top of it with the TV on for background noise.

Chapter 16

Nick woke up the next morning well rested. No dreams, no knocks on the door, no weird unexplainable things messing with him. He had the first restful night in a long time. That alone was refreshing. He got up off the couch and immediately noticed that every light in the apartment was on.

Nick giggled at himself for being scared last night and leaving the the lights on as he slept. It did give him some comfort, not being in the dark after everything that's been going on. But as he's recently learned, being in the light didn't necessarily protect one from the things that went bump in the night. Nevertheless, it gave him a sense of comfort, even if it was in vain.

Nick was feeling a bit nappy when he got up after sleeping in his clothes. He took a bath and cleaned himself up, putting on some clean clothes. The clothes he had on before had been worn for a couple of days as he moped around depressed.

But that wasn't going to happen today. Today was going to be a new breath of fresh air. Nothing was going to go wrong today nor was he going to allow anything to get him down.

He remembered Joe had asked him to come over this morning. Joe was sort of an early bird, so Nick knew he'd be up already. In fact, he's probably been up for a couple of hours already.

Nick picked up the strange book and thumbed through the pages. The writing definitely was weird and he wondered what language it was written in.

He wanted to show it to Joe again. Joe had only briefly thumbed through it and Nick don't think he really looked at it very closely. Maybe he'd recognize what language it was written in and maybe they could figure out what it said. With the dusty old book in hand, Nick walked over to Joe's apartment and knocked on the door.

Nick knocked and as usual, Joe yelled through the door.

"Come in!"

Nick opened the door and commented, "one day it's going to be a burglar or something at the door."

Joe laughed. "I knew it was you because I heard your door open and close. Then I heard you walking down the hall towards my apartment."

He noticed the book Nick was holding. "Did you get a chance to read that book and see what it's about?"

"No I haven't. It's written in some foreign language. I have no clue what it says."

He walked over and sat next to Joe while opening up the book to show him.

Joe's interest instantly sparked as he looked at it.

"I didn't really look at it very close last night. I didn't even notice how it was written. You found this in that empty apartment?"

"Yes."

After a moment of scanning through it, Joe said, "I think it's in some other language too but I don't know which language. I didn't recognize the characters."

"I wonder where it may have come from," Nick said.

"Nobody's rented that apartment since I've been here. In fact, I don't think anyone's rented that apartment at all since my uncle took over managing the place. Where exactly did you fins this? I've been in that apartment several times and never noticed it before."

"I just was bored and wandered in there. I sat on the floor for a bit, just hanging out I guess. That's when I seen it on the floor."

"I've never noticed that book before. Especially if it was just laying on the floor in the corner of the room, because I've vacuumed that apartment's carpet before. Maybe someone snuck in."

"Yeah, maybe. The door wasn't locked. I didn't notice it until I was just sitting there on the floor."

"Why were you just sitting on the floor in there?"

"I don't know, I just did. I was just bored I guess."

"Strange."

"That's not even the strange part. When I was sitting there, everything got dark around me and then out of nowhere, I noticed the book on the floor."

He looked at Nick and said, "wait a minute, everything went dark around you and this book was suddenly just there on the floor?"

"No, everything got dark around me and that's when I noticed the book setting there on the floor."

"Everything got dark? What do you mean?"

"I don't know." Nick said, "it's hard to describe and it may have just been nothing more then the sun setting."

He looked down at the pages in the book and then said, "look at these symbols that are written in it."

Nick looked and nodded.

"They look like witchcraft or something" he pointed out.

Nick looked again at the symbols Joe was pointing to and said, "so?"

"I bet they are" he said. "This is probably some demon thing."

At that remark Nick just laughed. "I seriously don't think it's some kind of demon book. You can tell it was handwritten by someone. Just because it's written in some other language we don't understand, doesn't make it evil."

"Dude, you don't understand," Joe tried to emphasize, "demons don't just appear in a puff of smoke and attack you like they do in the movies."

Joe was getting serious at this point. "They are beings that live in a whole different realm or plane than we do."

Nick gave him a look and raised his eyebrow skeptically.

"They get into your head, drive you insane and make you destroy everything meaningful around you."

Nick made no comment.

"Think about it," he rationalized. "Why would a demon appear before you and mess with you like they do in the movies?"

Nick shrugged his shoulders.

"If they are trying to steer you away from God then that would be going about it the wrong way. If a demon suddenly showed up and started fucking with you then the first thing you're going to do is run to the nearest church and become the most devote Christian there ever was or whatever."

"Sure, I get what you're saying."

"You see. they try to get into your head and you don't even know they're there and then they slowly drive you insane."

Nick laughed and said, "dude, you're trying to get into

MY head."

They both laughed, then Joe said, "we should take this book to that occult book store."

"What occult book store?"

"There's an occult book store a few blocks down the road," he replied. "I bet they would know what the writing and symbols in that book mean."

"Well you do have my curiosity stirred up a bit now," Nick said smiling. "Do you think they're open?"

"I bet they are, let's go check it out, we can take my car." With that resolution in mind, Joe stood up and grabbed his keys that were setting on his coffee table.

Nick looked up at him laughing and said, "just like that, you're up and ready." Laughing even harder, he pointed out, "with keys in hand he's ready to go and solve the mystery."

"Yep, and it didn't even require a single Scooby snack. I'm ready," Joe laughed and said, "grab the book and let's go check it out."

Nick got up and grabbed the old book, following Joe out of the apartment. He locked the door behind him and Nick followed him out to the main stairwell outside. They walked around the corner to where Joe had parked his car.

Joe walked around to the driver's side and opened his door while saying, "get in, it's unlocked."

He drove them a few blocks down the street to a small

occult book store that was located on a small business strip. He parked the car in front and Nick looked over at the book store's storefront. It was painted dark violet and purple with pentagrams, dragons, and various other occult type symbols painted randomly here and there.

He looked over at Joe and said, "are you sure you wanna go in there? It looks like some kind of satanic place or something."

Joe looked at the building and laughed. "Naw dude, it's not. It's cool. They sell all kinds of books with different beliefs and religious practices."

"Oh, how do you know?"

"I've been in there a couple of times and bought some incense. It's where I got that cool crystal dragon that's in my kitchen window.

Nick knew of the crystal dragon he was referring to. He shown it to him when he first bought it a couple of months ago when Nick came over to visit. It would reflect cool rainbow spots on the wall when the sun hit it just right.

"Ah, so this is where you got it."

"Yeah, I got it here." he said as he opened the car door to get out. "Come on, you gotta check this place out. It has a lot of cool things in there," he added as he got out of the car.

Nick opened the door on his side of the car and got out, shutting the door behind him.

Joe quickly said, "hey, don't forget to grab the book."

Realizing he left it in the car seat, Nick grabbed the old book out of the car. Carrying it with him as he stepped up on the curb and joined Joe entering the book store.

The inside of the occult book store was dimly lit. It took a moment for their eyes to adjust to it. The scent of incense flooded the senses asthey came in. It originated from a variety of incense sticks that were on a display rack near the entrance. Nick and Joe walked in and began looking around. The overwhelming scent of the mixed incense left as they walked further inside where the smell of burnt apple cinnamon became more dominant.

Most likely the scent they had burning in the corner near the register where a woman in her mid forties sat behind the counter. She had two-toned hair that had been dyed in alternating strips of either blonde or black and she wore a long black dress with a black shawl over her shoulders.

Nick smirked when he considered that she was probably dressing the part to fit the occult bookstore's theme.

"Can I help you find anything?" she asked.

Joe turned and looked at the woman, who had now walked around the counter and was approaching them.

"Sure, but I'm not sure if you can help us or not." he said.

The woman stood next to Joe and said, "oh I don't know, what is it that I can help you boys with?"

Joe walked over to Nick and took the old book he was holding and showed it to her.

"He found this old book and it looks like it was written by hand in some kind of weird ancient language."

She took the book out of Joe's hands and set it down on top of a glass cabinet display that was filled with various decks of tarot cards.

Joe then said, "it has a lot of symbols in it, we figured it probably has something to do with the occult."

She examined the outside cover, "You can tell that it's made the old school way. That it wasn't made by any printing machine."

She opened it and said, "oh yes, you can tell it is all hand made and handwritten. It looks like they even made the paper for the pages themselves too."

She carefully turned the pages, examining them as she did and then came to a page that had writing on it and said, "oh, I see the writing you're talking about."

She turned a couple more pages and looked at the writing and said, "it looks like it's written in ancient Etruscan or maybe Phoenician."

She flipped around the pages some more and looked at some of the symbols that were drawn in it. She pointed at one of them and said, "I definitely recognize this symbol, it's an old Norse protection symbol."

She went through the pages until she got to the blank pages and said "yeah, it looks like it was a work in progress. It's probably somebody's unfinished spell book."

She got to the page near the end that was written in English and said, "this part is written in English. So yeah, I would say you found someone's spell book. It's probably written in English using an alphabet only the writer knows. All you really have to do is break its code and you can read it"

"You can take some of the known descriptions, like the symbols and other things like direction to help decipher it." Joe added.

"Yeah, good idea. The book and its writings are not meant for anyone's eyes except the writer's. There's no telling what alphabet they made up for it."

"What alphabet?" Nick asked.

"Using personal made up alphabets was a typical practice of wizards, witches, sorcerers, and other practitioners of magick," she tried to explain.

"Why would they do that?" he asked.

"It was to protect themselves from religious persecution." she said bluntly. "If you remember correctly, they used to burn witches. Anyone practicing magic or any kind of divination would do their best to keep it secret."

Nick and Joe nodded.

"One method was to write their grimoires or their spells and any other instructions in a alphabet or language that only they understood and nobody else."

"They kept the fact that they even had a spell book a secret and they carefully kept their writings in it hidden from the eyes of everyone." she added.

"Wow. We definitely have a puzzle to solve." Nick said.

"I can offer you store credit for the book if you're interested in selling it." she said.

"Thanks, but I am way too curious about it now to trade or sell it."

Joe and Nick looked around in the store a bit. After a little shopping, Joe purchased a couple of books and some incense sticks prior to leaving.

Nick didn't want to spend any money unnecessarily until he at least found a job. Joe's curiosity about the book had grown as much as Nick's and he even offered to trade him for it.

On their way home they made a brief stop at a drive-thru restaurant. When they returned to the apartment building, Nick parted ways with Joe because he said that he had to get ready for work.

Nick wanted to work on trying to decipher the book and after eating the take out food they picked up on our way back, he set to work on deciphering the dusty old book.

He took the lady at the occult book store's advice and started trying to decipher the author's alphabet by using the diagram of a protection circle. Armed with a notebook and pencil, he worked on deciphering the old book.

After a few hours, he managed to unraveled a few

letters and discovered that it indeed had been written in English. This made further deciphering easier. It would probably take a few days of decoding until he would be able to read much of it. There were still a few letters he couldn't figure out, which left quite a few words unknown. Entire sentences were unreadable without more of the letters being deciphered.

However, he was still able to read some of it. It was as that lady had described it probably would be. The personal notes and step by step spell instructions of a witch or wizard. Some parts listed out names and words he wasn't able to decipher yet. Most were on symbols and rituals. It seemed like it was indeed someone's personal hand written spell book.

Nick found the book to be very interesting. Much of the subject matter he had to look up at the local library or from books that he later got from the occult book store. He began to submerge himself in absorbing various kinds of occult knowledge to keep his mind off of Laura.

Nick had pretty much isolated himself from the rest of the world, immersing himself in the book's writings.

Chapter 17

After Nick studied the dusty old spell book for a number of days, he felt that he had a fairly good run down on the basics of what was written within its pages. Not that he was now an expert in the occult or anything. But from what he could decipher from the book, it seemed to cover pretty much of what he'd already been reading in other books on the subject.

The majority of what was written in it seemed to deal with protecting oneself from a variety of things. Evil things, other spell casters, and pretty much anyone or anything that meant harm.

There was still a lot of knowledge missing from the book. As if there were two books and the book that he found was primarily the writer's book of protections. Nick came to the conclusion that there had to be another book. He wanted to find it and believed that it was probably somewhere in that vacant apartment. He decided to go search for it.

He went back into the vacant apartment where he found the book. It felt cold inside the apartment. Even though the evening still held the humid air that lingered from the day, it was cold in there. Just as before, the apartment was still dimly lit from the street lights that came in from the outside. The corners of the room were darkened in shadow and it made him feel very uneasy inside the apartment.

He had an apprehensive feeling that was telling him to get out of there. His raging curiosity drove him forward. He had to see if there was anything else left behind by whoever wrote the book. Perhaps another book, some notes or something else useful. There had to be another book or something left behind.

When Nick looked in the direction of the kitchen area leading into the bathroom, he could hear something moving around in the dark.

Something was in the darkened bathroom hallway.

He could sense it and even feel it there. He looked into the darkness where he'd heard the sounds. The floor squeaked like someone was shifting their weight back there. The floor squeaked again and he could tell someone was coming out from the dark bathroom hallway.

Someone was definitely there. The floor squeaked again and Nick could see someone in the darkened corridor slowly stepping forward. It was a shadowed silhouette of someone standing back there hiding in darkness of the hallway.

"Hello?" he called out, "who's there?"

Nick strained to see who it was in the darkness, but all he could see was their shadowed silhouette in the doorway.

It was a person. And then he heard his name said.

A weak and faint *"Nick."*

Nick was too nervous to approach whoever or whatever just stood there concealed in the darkness.

"Who is there?"

He heard his name being said again, *"Nick?"*

It sounded familiar, like Laura's voice.

Uncertain and puzzled he replied back, "Laura? Is that you back there?"

Not wanting to step into the uncertain darkness that cloaked the hallway, Nick remained standing in the partially illuminated living room. He looked at the figure in the shadows as it started to walk towards him from the back room. He could tell it was a person, but still couldn't tell who it was until they came closer into the light.

The figure slowly walked closer and came into the light. Nick was able to make out who it was. It was Laura.

Nick's heart began to pound as fear tried to overcome him. He felt light headed and his hands began to sweat and tremble.

This was all wrong.

Something deep in his mind told him that it was not Laura standing there. It looked and sounded exactly like her, but it was not her. He knew she would not be hiding in the darkness of a dirty vacant apartment.

Nick looked at her as she slowly walked closer towards him. She was barefooted. He also noticed that not only was she barefooted, but her feet were blackened and filthy. Her hair was down and partially covering her face. She kept her head slightly bowed down looking at the ground while she walked towards him. Almost as if she was wary of coming too close and letting him see her face clearly.

This all felt wrong. Something inside him was in panic and telling him to run and run now!

Nick took a step back and the moment he did, she stopped approaching and just stood there. She lifted her head up and looked at him. It was Laura, but it wasn't. Her eyes were wrong. They were all black!

As soon as he seen her eyes, he gasped and took a step back. Nick was instantly overcome with fear. He quickly looked around the room towards the door wanting to run away. But he couldn't get out without stepping past her or whatever it was. His eyes burned and watered. He felt like he wanted to cry out in fear and throw up at the same time. He was trapped and had no idea what this thing was. All he knew was that he was very afraid of it.

He could feel the coldness of its hatred chilling the room around him. It stood there looking like Laura, but with black soulless eyes that stared, not at him, but into him.

Nick didn't know what to do. He knew he was in great peril. He had to get away from it somehow. He had to get out of there.

Looking at the old windows in the living room, for just a

270

brief moment, he considered jumping out through them. But the windows weren't very big and had solid wood frames. He really didn't think he'd be able to smash through them like the gunslingers in one of those old western movies. Not forgetting they were on the second floor.

Having no escape or any other option and suddenly gaining a spine, Nick turned towards it and demanded, "what are you!"

"What do you want from me!?"

It didn't answer. It just stood there partially cloaked in the room's shadows. Nick knew something was wrong. All of this wasn't right. It started to step back away from him towards the darker part of the room. The room's shadows seemed to grow darker and larger. Nick held his ground. After all, he didn't really have anywhere to run to anyways.

"Who are you?" he demanded again.

She backed away from him even further into the shadows and seemed to almost disappear into the darkness within the corner of the room.

Nick could still faintly see its blackened form within the darkness in the corner of the room. He tried to imagine it being pushed back away. To be pushed back and pinned into the corner.

To his surprise, it seemed to be working.

He felt he was able to hold it in place by some kind of force that he seemed to borrow from the energy that was around the room itself. He didn't know how, but he was able to draw from it and focus it enough to pin this thing into the corner of the wall. Nick didn't know how he was doing it, but he wasn't going to question it at this point.

He knew this thing he was pinning to the corner was something other than what it had appeared to be. It definitely was not Laura. It was something else. He now wondered if this had been the thing that he thought was Laura that one night. Whatever this thing was, it was something that did not belong here. He remembered what he'd read in that old book about circles of protection.

He envisioned an invisible circle being formed around him. He closed his eyes and imagined an intensely bright and powerful circle of light forming around him. So complete and perfect was this circle, nothing could penetrate it. An exceptional force around him like a bubble that nothing could enter. Within it, he knew he was safe from everything. He kept his eyes tightly closed as he continued to imagine this bright white circle that was formed around him.

In his mind, he envisioned the darkness itself forming to his will. The density of it becoming even denser and thicker until it began to take form. First as just a density of darkness, then as a floating dark mist.

He could feel this thing's eyes on him, staring at him from the dark corner where it was pinned with it's hatred. But this time he felt something different from it. He felt its fear of him.

Yes, it was definitely fear. It was afraid of him.

272

Nick concentrated and manipulated the growing swirling tails of darkness around and started to wrap them around it. The swirling mists constricted as they twisted around it like snakes coming from every direction of the shadows.

The shadows wrapped around it tighter and tighter. Nick felt that the energy was apart of him and he envisioned it squeezing even tighter. Wrapping as tight as they could. He tightly closed his eyes and tensed up his body. His fists were balled up tight as he gripped them even tighter.

He envisioned squeezing this thing pinned to the corner even tighter until nothing remained to squeeze and then he let out a loud roaring yell as he looked up and flung his arms out, releasing the energy in a giant climax.

There was an explosion of force around Nick. He felt it pull every ounce of energy out of his body. A source of energy that seemed to come from somewhere deep within him.

Nick dropped to the floor, exhausted and drained. His head dizzily spun as he fell to the ground in a lump of spent flesh. He was so tired that he couldn't even hold his eyes open.

He was so very tired. All he wanted was to sleep.

But he was afraid to sleep. He couldn't put his guard down and leave himself open to whatever else was out there. But he couldn't continue anymore. He no longer cared, he was too tired. His eyes were already closed. He could feel his eyes trying to close even more as exhaustion sank him into the welcoming blissfulness of sleep.

He desperately tried to resist. He had to get back up, but he was too tired. He couldn't even imagine existing anymore, he only wanted sleep. Just to rest for a few moments. Just long enough to replenish and then he could get up.

Suddenly, he heard the apartment door burst open.

He didn't even bother looking to see who it was. He was simply too exhausted to look or care.

Within an instant, he heard a loud explosion and was suddenly blinded by an intense bright light. A light so intense that he couldn't tell the difference if his eyes were open or shut. Within that very moment, everything became quiet around him. Everything was muffled as if he was cupping his ears closed or was wearing earplugs. The only thing he could hear was an intense ringing sound that seemed to come from the center of his head.

The air around him seemed like it was choking him too.

His vision slowly came back and all he could see was an intense blind spot in his eyes from the previous flash of bright light just a second ago.

It became even harder to breathe as it seemed like his throat didn't want the air around him and was refusing it. It burned and made him cough uncontrollably. Nick could see a haze around him that looked like smoke encircling him.

274

Piercing through the smoky haze came a hail of light beams danced around around him. They came from the doorway. There were shadows behind the dancing lights.

Nick felt weak as his muscles went limp, feeling exhausted as his body seemed to lock up on the floor, almost like in a seizure or convulsion. He had no control over his body. His eyes and nose burned as he choked in the smoke.

Suddenly, there was a burst of intense white light that went directly into his eyes. And then nothing.

Chapter 18

Nurse Sally Ratchet had worked at the Care Center for about eleven years. She had started working there as an orderly. Something they call Certified Nurses Aides now. CNA for short. While she started working there, she had taken some classes and finished some of her education and now worked there as a practical nurse.

She worked mostly on the East wing where the mental ward was located, but often worked where the administrative staff needed her. Sally's kids were now grown and had all made their way out of the nest. Her schedule was now much more flexible than it had been in previous years when she had to be home for her kids.

Today she was working on the East wing with a new nurse that she was suppose to help train. She really didn't mind training new people. But most that showed up for the job really didn't know what they were getting into and didn't last at all.

Many new people would disappear completely during their first lunch break. There had been several occasions when she had seen people that had taken their lunch break, clocked out for their thirty minute lunch break and never show up again. Some new staff members would last just long enough to get a paycheck and then they were gone forever as well.

It was depressing work that was often laborious and offered only low wages and almost no fringe benefits. It was not exactly employment for the career minded. On top of all of that, working on the East wing required additional attention to detail. It was kept separate from the rest of the care facility that housed predominately elderly and retired individuals that required long term intermediate care. Some for long term care recovery and some were there for care indefinitely.

The East wing housed the mental patients of various ages and disorders. Some of them were very dangerous and kept sedated while kept on restraints at all times. Even the ones that were ambulatory, were still kept sedated and under some kind of restraint.

The entire wing was locked off as well. The access door automatically shut and locked. It required a card key and a four digit code to open the door. These mental patients were deemed dangerous to themselves and society and were never to be allowed in the general public. Some of them had committed heinous crimes and have been kept under sedation by order of the courts. This was where the really crazy and dangerous people really end up.

This corridor was nicknamed by the staff as the hall of zombies. The individuals housed there were so heavily sedated that they merely existed in flesh alone. Most slept nearly all the time and those that did show a minute sign of consciousness had only blank and empty catatonic stares. They were there in body only, but not in mind. Their minds had been shut off through the pharmaceutical magic of modern biochemistry. In this hall, the patients were usually kept restrained in their beds. Most were tended to by staff as the patient laid in bed, often asleep and oblivious to anything around them.

Some of the lucky patients were often placed in wheelchairs and parked in the hallway. When the weather permitted, they would open the central barred window and allow fresh air in. This benefited everyone as not only did the patients fortunate enough to get strapped in a wheelchair and rolled into the hallway had the advantage of getting some sunshine and fresh air, the staff benefited from the opened window as well.

As these patients all required a high level of personal care, there was always the putrid odor of urine and fecal matter that tended to linger in the air at all times, no matter the efforts of the housekeeping staff to combat it.

It was fifteen minutes past nine o'clock and the new girl she was suppose to be training to work in this hall had not shown up yet. She was already late and was already getting off to a bad start.

Sally didn't have time to wait around any longer. They will just have to hire someone a little more punctual and dependable is all. She had to start the late morning patient rounds, new trainee in tow or not. Sally got up from the hard fiberglass chair she had been sitting in and tossed the empty styrofoam cup she had been drinking coffee from that she had got from the facility's lunch room into the plastic lined trash receptacle by the door.

She gathered her medicine cart and began to go down the hallway to the first patient's room. Each room had two beds and two patients in it. Two rooms would share a toilet facility that linked the two together. They were never used, as even though most of the patients were ambulatory, they were kept under sedation and generally could not move on their own without assistance anyways.

Sally pushed the medicine cart down the hall towards the first patients room. It had a bad wheel on it that squeaked horribly as she wheeled it around. "Squweeeep, squweeep, squeep, squeep, squeep, squeep" the wheel squeaked out as she pushed it down the hall, announcing her coming.

She heard thunder blast outside really loud and the lights flickered for a second. She looked down the hall out the window and could see that it was still storming really hard. It was probably why the new girl was late. She, herself had some issues getting to work as the wind blew her around in her car as she drove to work this morning.

Just as Sally had got her med cart wheeled to the first door in the hall, she heard a knocking on the main door leading to the East wing.

She looked over and seen someone waving in the door window.

"It's probably the new girl," she thought.

280

They wouldn't give her a key card yet or an access code until they knew for sure that the new girl would work out and stay. Sally looked down at her cart and made sure it was still locked. It contained a variety of prescription medicines for the patients and had to be kept under lock and key at all times. It was fairly way too common occurrence for a nursing facility's medicine cart to be robbed by staff members of it's drugs by various secret drug abusers. Seeing the cart was still locked and secured, she turned to walk down the hall and let the new girl in.

Sally took the key card she had hanging on a cord from around her neck that her granddaughter had made for her and swiped the keypad with it. She then proceeded to punch in the digital key combination and the door buzzed open as soon as she did so.

The girl waiting on the other side pulled the door open.

"Are you Sally Ratchet?" she asked.

"Yes, I'm Sally Ratchet. Are you the new girl that was suppose to be here?"

"Yes, I'm sorry I'm a little bit late. The rain slowed me down. I get nervous driving in it."

"What's your name?"

"Donna Mitchel."

"Well, Donna, let's get started." Sally led her down the hall to where her medicine cart was parked and explained how the hallway worked and that the door to the wing had to remain closed and locked at times, no matter what.

She informed the new girl that she would get her own key card with her own key code with a photo on it like hers from the administrator in a day or two. Otherwise, Sally explained, she would have to hit the red button on the wall by the door to have someone let her in or out. Security had to be maintained and the doors never left open for any reason. There was always the chance that without warning, one of the patients could come out of their sedation and get out. Donna raised her eyebrows, looking a bit concerned.

Sally informed her that she would always have to stay alert when working in these halls. That most of the patients sedated on this wing were here because they were a danger to themselves and everyone around them. They weren't fit to be locked up in prison and they were much too dangerous to be in a regular mental facility.

Donna asked her why.

"It's the State's solution for the dangerously insane or criminally dangerous. This is the States solution to their problem as to what to do about these people."

"Really?"

"They found that it was more economical to sedate them and keep them confined inside secured nursing homes."

Donna gasped. She had never heard anything like this before. It really wasn't something she had given much thought to before. It made some sense in a sort of warped way, but she did kind of rationalize with what Sally was saying. After all, what do you do with them.

Sally continued to explain that she'd have to stay alert in

case any patient came out of sedation and if they did that they could physically attack. She also told Donna that certain patients must always be kept in restraints. She explained that this is why she had to get a police background check before she was allowed to work on this wing, That essentially, they were also prison guards. Some of them are real bad schizophrenics that harm themselves.

"The guy down the hall," Sally pointed with the pen that she held her hand and looked over her glasses down the hall towards one of the room doors and said, "there's a guy in that room that starts viciously biting himself the very moment he comes out of sedation."

She pointed out, "he doesn't just bite himself, he literally bites chunks out of his arm and even chews his own lips."

Donna was horrified to hear this.

Sally then said, "you can see on his arms where they have grafted parts of his skin back on and where parts of his lips are missing."

She then pushed her med cart into the room they were standing by and continued explaining, "yeah, he's one we keep sedated at all times and have to tube feed."

She added, "he hurts himself every time he's brought of sedation."

As the med cart that Sally pushed made it's squeal each time the little wheel made a revolution, Donna asked, "wow, does that thing squeak like that all the time?"

Sally laughed and said, "yeah, it's been doing it since

last year."

She then remarked, "they put oil on it to try to make it stop squeaking, but it didn't work and squeaks all the time anyways."

"I sort of just got used to it," she added, "I only have to push it around to each room three times a shift anyways."

As they came into the room, she explained to Donna to make sure the patient in this room was always be on restraints and sedated. She explained, that the red tag on the end of his bed meant that he was 'State Ward' and a danger to those around him.

Donna asked Sally what, 'State Ward' meant.

Sally replied by stating that they were the criminally insane that the State kept restrained and sedated. She pointed out, "just remember, red tag means a red flag. Make sure they are restrained and sedated at all times."

Sally then walked over to the head of the bed and turn on the light that hung over it.

The patient lying there, jerked momentarily as she clicked the light on.

This made Donna jump a little, whom was not expecting the patient to move after just hearing that they were dangerous.

Sally noticed her jump and said, "don't worry, he's secured in place."

She then went on saying, "some of them will be awake

when you go into their room, you will have to get used to it and always be on your guard."

"This guy tends to jerk a little when you turn on the light." Then she said, "this guy here, he's the guy that had killed his that girl a couple years ago."

Donna questioned, "killed his girlfriend?"

Sally replied, "yeah, he's the guy that was on the news that mutilated that girl and killed those other people."

Donna gasped, looking down at the patient that was lying there, strapped in the hospital bed in front of them and said, "that's him?"

"I remember hearing about that on the news. Isn't she still missing because they never were able to identify the body or something like that?"

"Nope, I heard there really wasn't a body. What they had were mutilated body parts all of over the corner of the wall."

Donna gasp. She looked horrified.

"They really couldn't identify any of it except that they knew that it was human, because all the blood tested as being all human. The floor was drenched in blood with small chunks of flesh everywhere,.. except in one strange spot."

"What? How do you know all this?" Donna asked.

Sally explained, "well, my nephew was one of the cops that went in and he said when they entered the apartment looking for this guy and found him laying spread out in the middle of the floor with a perfect circle around him that was clean."

"What do you mean by clean?"

"My nephew said it was weird. That it looked there had been some kind of barrier or something around the guy that kept the blood off."

"Why do they think happened?"

"He thin maybe they guy used a kiddie pool or something, but they never found anything. But because the rest of the floor had blood spilled and splattered everywhere, they think he used something to shield it."

"So he smeared blood everywhere, but that one spot?"

"He said it was all over the floors and walls like someone had exploded in a million pieces, except for a perfect circle that was around this guy on the floor."

"Now that's weird."

"They said that a circle around this guy was totally clean of any blood or anything. So they thin he was shielded or covered under something."

"It's troubling to think someone would do such an incredibly insane thing like that."

"The guy was spotless, that's the reason he's in here," she pointed out, "they aren't sure if he even did it. From what my nephew said, they just found him there laying on the floor when the S.W.A.T. Team burst in."

"Laying on the floor?"

"They said that he was barely conscious and was unresponsive."

Donna was horrified upon hearing this all be described to her and even more horrified that this was the guy she remembered hearing about in the news. She wasn't so sure about this job anymore, if it were even a safe place to work. After all, what happens if this guy wakes up and comes out of his restraints. How many others that were like him that were here, she wondered.

'So,... they aren't even sure of this guy is the killer or a victim that may have survived?" Donna asked.

"That's right, except for one thing.

"What's that?"

"The SWAT team were already coming to apprehend him. My nephew said he was the primary suspect to a couple murders and they'd been searching for him."

"How'd they find him?"

"His landlord got suspicious of him and then seen on the news that he was wanted in question of those homicides. So I guess he called them."

"So the police have absolutely no clue what all really happened or what he was even doing in there?" Donna asked.

"That girl is still considered missing because they really don't have a body that they can really identify as being her or not. All they have is lots and lots of blood. So yeah, the police are unsure if he is a crime scene victim or if he is the one who did it."

Donna shook her head in disbelief.

"From what I am told, they were already looking for him. Apparently there was some kind of love triangle thing going on. They had found her boyfriend's body in a dumpster the day after they found a body in the same dumpster the day before."

"So it's probably him."

"Yeah, they were already looking for him in connection with those bodies they found in the dumpster. My nephew said the only reason they showed with SWAT was because the landlord said the guy scared him and he wasn't sure if he was armed or not."

"So they weren't taking any chances."

"Law enforcement is a very dangerous job, who can blame them."

"Wait a second, then why is he here?"

"The court felt it was best to keep him sedated here until he comes out of whatever's wrong with him and then maybe he can someday tell them what happened. Or at least until the police figure it out on their own."

"How is he suppose to come out of it when he's kept sedated 24/7 ?"

"That is beyond me."

Donna shook her head. "That's just crazy."

"That's not all that's crazy. I didn't quite believe it all when I first heard it." Sally hesitated a moment. "But here's where it gets even weirder."

She stepped over and pulled away the sheet that was covering the body of the patient that laid on the bed facing the window. He just laid there and seemingly staring blankly into nothingness with glossed over eyes.

"Look at his skin closely," Sally said to Donna as she bent down closer to look herself. "See the markings?" She asked, motioning for Donna to look closer, "look at this, there is some kind of faint weird writing or inscriptions all over his body"

Donna bent down and looked closer, seeing the marking that ran across the patient's body. The faint gray writing trailed in lines that went in different directions and snaked all around his body.

"If you look really close, you can see that it's like they aren't tattoos at all. They look like they are actually under his skin," Sally pointed out.

"It looks as if they were written under his skin," Donna said as she looked closer at the tranquilized patient's back and arms. She could see the inscriptions running all over his body under his skin.

"They sort of look like they are faded tattoos, but they do appear to look like they are actually under his skin," Donna said.

Sally added, "its as if you have to look really close to even see them."

Sally stood up straight and said, "they don't have any of it listed on his report for identifying marks or tattoos."

Donna looked up at her puzzled.

She explained, "the patients will have write ups to identify them. Such things as their race, hair and eye color, and any identifying marks."

Donna nodded and said, "and so?"

Sally said, "They don't have these marks listed on his body."

"Maybe they didn't notice them," Donna remarked.

"Maybe, but it's odd," pointed out Sally.

Donna looked at the inscriptions across his back and remarked, "wow, what was he, some kind of religious fanatic, cult member or something?"

Sally laughed, "no, I don't think so. If he was, I have never seen anything like that before."

"They look like some kind of ancient writing, maybe he's covered in spells or something," she jokingly said.

"I don't know," said Donna, "it doesn't look like it's written on him as much as seems like it is written *in* him."

"Wow, that's a creepy thought," remarked Sally and then she pulled the sheet back over him and covered him up once again.

Sally leaned closer to Donna and said, "nobody believes me when I say this, but I think they move on him too."

"What?!" gasped Donna.

"Yeah, if you look at them one day and come back and look at them again on the next day, they look different. Maybe it's my eyes, but they look like they slowly shifted on his body or something."

Donna looked at her in disbelief and said, "nuh uh, you're just messing with me."

"He doesn't have any property that we know of, we really know nothing about him."

Looking down on him, she said, "this is exactly how he arrived here."

Donna seemed uncomfortable, so Sally changed the conversation from gossip back to training.

"Okay, you have nothing to worry about this guy and he's easy to care for. He just has to be turned every few hours and make sure his vitals are stable. Other than hygiene and changing bedding, he's to be kept sedated."

Sally pulled up the chart she had on the medicine cart and showed Donna where his medicine schedules were and what he was to be given. She explained how the chart worked then got out her keys and unlocked one of the trays on the cart. She removed a syringe with a pre-measured injection dose contained in it.

"He's to start his day with one of these." She said while unwrapping the package it was sealed in.

She reached down and pulled the cover back down, exposing his thigh and injected him with the contents of the syringe.

"Make sure you always put the used needles in the 'sharps container' after use." Sally said as she disposed the used syringe into the red sharps container that was attached on top of the medicine cart that she was pushing around.

She covered him back up and turned off the light. With her trainee in tow behind her, she squeaked the med cart out of the room.

As they walked, she explained that each patient was to get their perspective injections the very first thing in the morning when she was to start her shift. That it was very important that it took place without fail before she began her other duties. It was their daily sedation and that it could not be forgotten if she wanted to not lose control of the wing and get somebody hurt. She pointed out, that not all the patients were dangerous, but it was best to assume so until she got to know each patient on the wing.

Chapter 19

He laid there staring out into the nothingness. The attacking light had just left after stinging him again and making his whole body tingle with that strange taste in his mouth.

He heard the shadows whispering amongst themselves again. His tormentors that came with the light that would bring its pain. He heard the bird call out its usual warning, but the light wasn't immediate as usual, even though it did eventually come to attack.

He couldn't tell if he was dreaming or not. If he dreamt anything he never remembered it. He felt ill to his stomach from the feeling going through his body from the insect's sting. It made every muscle in his body limp and turn into putty. Almost as if he wasn't even in a body.

He just looked out into nothingness. Everything was hazy. His eyes were getting heavy and he could feel himself slipping away again.

He could hear them coming closer and calling him. The wind howled out his name in the distance.

Nick Runarstein was held at the Oklahoma Forensic Center located in Vinita, Ok which housed 200 patients who are either seeking treatment for competency, or found "not guilty by reason of insanity" (NGRI). These patients were receiving treatment at this secured facility so they can be competent to stand trial.

The property is now deserted and condemned; the last patients having been moved out in 2008.

Many of the 'patients' were relocated to smaller facilities across the state, mostly in nursing homes equipped to facilitate patients with mental illnesses requiring extensive care.

During this period of time, Nick Runarstein had become lost in the shuffle of facility transfers. Authorities have been unable to locate him or verify whether they still have him in custody or not.

He has been missing since 2009.

Anyone having knowledge of his location are advised to call CrimeStoppers.

9 781943 066216